PAY THE TOLL

In a whine of engines and a blue cloud of oil smoke, a half dozen four-wheelers broke out of the trees and raced alongside us. Two of them, ones I hadn't seen in Rock Lake, were driven by larger guys; plastic rifle scabbards jutted from the rear.

"Keep going!" I shouted to my family.

The gang matched our pace, then sped ahead. I thought they were leaving—until they turned sharply, skidded to a stop, and blocked the highway. We had nowhere to go.

And the *Ali Princess* had no real brakes.

"Drag your feet!" I cried. We did, and managed to stop just inches short of a muddy, battered vehicle with balloon tires.

"What is this?" my mother said. As usual, she hopped off the *Ali Princess* and stepped forward.

"This is a toll road," the biggest driver said. He glanced to the others, who nodded. I looked again at the rifle scabbards.

"No, it's a public highway," my mother said.

"Not today it isn't."

ALSO BY WILL WEAVER

The Survivors:
THE SEQUEL TO MEMORY BOY

Claws

Billy Baggs books:

Hard Ball

Farm Team

Striking Out

WILL
WEAVER

MEMORY BOY

An Imprint of HarperCollinsPublishers

The excerpts that appear on pages 22–24 are reprinted with the permission of Scribner, a Division of Simon & Schuster, from *Ring of Fire* by David Ritchie. Copyright © 1981 by David Ritchie.

HarperTeen is an imprint of HarperCollins Publishers.

Memory Boy
Copyright © 2001 by Will Weaver
Library of Congress Cataloging-in-Publication Data
Weaver, Will.
    Memory Boy/a novel by Will Weaver.
        p.   cm.
    Summary: Sixteen-year-old Miles and his family must flee their Minneapolis home and begin a new life in the wilderness after a chain of cataclysmic volcanic explosions creates dangerous conditions in the city.
    ISBN 978-0-06-201814-4
    1. Wilderness survival—Fiction.   2. Family life—Fiction.]   I. Title.
PZ7.W3623Me   2001   00-32049
[Fic]—dc21   CIP
                                                                                       AC

Typography by Erin Fitzsimmons
11 12 13 14 15   CG/BV   10 9 8 7 6 5 4 3 2 1
❖
Revised edition, 2012

CONTENTS

CHAPTER ONE

NOW OR NEVER

IT WAS THE PERFECT TIME for leaving. Weather conditions were finally right: a steady breeze blew from the south, plus there was just enough moonlight to see by.

July 3, 2008.

This would be the date our family would always remember, assuming, of course, that we lived to tell about it.

"Hurry up. The wind won't last forever," I said. Three shadowy figures—my sister, Sarah, and my parents—fumbled with their luggage. With me, we were the Newell family. We lived in west suburban Minneapolis—for a few more minutes, at least.

"Shut up, Miles," Sarah muttered. She was twelve going on thirteen, and her carry-on bag overflowed with last-minute additions. I couldn't complain; I had my own private stuff, including a small sealed jar that would be hard to explain to my family. So I didn't try. Right now one of Sarah's stupid paperbacks dropped with a thud onto the sidewalk. I sighed and went to help her.

"I'm not leaving," Sarah said, jerking away from me. "Everybody's going to die anyway, so why can't we die in our own house?" She plopped down onto the lawn. Pale pumice puffed up around her and hung in the air like a ghostly double. That was the weird thing about the volcanic ash; it had been falling softly, softly falling, for over two years now—and sometimes it was almost beautiful. Tonight the rock flour suspended in the air made a wide, furry-white halo around the moon. Its giant, raccoon-like eyeball stared down and made the whole neighborhood look X-rayed.

"Nobody's going to die," I said. "Though if we stay in the city, we might," I muttered to myself.

"How do you know?" Sarah said. She sat there stubbornly, clutching her elbows.

"Actually, I don't. Which is why we're leaving."

Sarah swore at me. Anything logical really pissed her off these days.

"Arthur!" my mother said sharply to my father. "Help out anytime."

My father coughed briefly and stepped forward. "Think of it this way, Sarah. We're heading to the lake," he said, his voice muffled under his dust mask. "We'll get to our cabin, kick back, ride this out. Swiss Family Robinson all the way." He manufactured a short laugh that fell about fifty yards short of sincere. Sometimes I worried more about him than my sister and mother; they at least knew how to put wood in a fireplace. My father was a real city guy, a musician, a jazz drummer.

My mother added, "We all agreed, remember? As Miles said, up at Birch Bay we'll have more control of things, like heat, food, and water. When things improve—when the ash stops falling, and when there's gasoline, and when the food stores are full again—we'll come back home." Something, maybe the dust, caught briefly in her throat.

"Miles said we'll have to stay up there all winter and all next year—maybe longer," Sarah said.

My parents were silent. They looked at each other. My father shrugged.

"What does Miles know?" Sarah said loudly. "He's barely sixteen! Why are we listening to him?"

"Can we not wake the neighbors?" I whispered urgently.

Sarah swore at me, and suddenly we were arguing like children.

"Enough!" my mother said to us. Natalie—everybody knows her as Nat, which is a good name because she's small and intense—reached down and yanked Sarah to her feet. "Think of it like . . . a vacation. Maybe a little longer than usual, but still a vacation."

"Or better, pretend you're Mary Poppins," I said to Sarah. "When the wind was right, up, up, and away she went!"

"Miles," Nat said in warning. She looked to my father for help; he turned away, to his small duffel bag, and checked its zipper. Typical. Even though he was home nowadays, most of the time it still felt like he was gone.

Me, I had work to do. I went to the garage and eased up the big door. Inside sat my supreme invention of all time: the *Ali Princess*. I rolled her outside, and in the moonlight she was beautiful.

Perched on her six bicycle wheels, the *Ali Princess* looked like a gigantic grasshopper poised to spring away at first touch—or a dragonfly ready to take flight. Down her center, like an exoskeleton, was a bicycle built for two. The tandem bike with in-line, recumbent seats had belonged to my parents. It was one of those high-priced, spend-quality-time-together gifts that my father had bought for my mother. I had seen them together on it maybe once; the bike didn't have five miles on it. Attached to the main bike, like legs on a water-strider bug, were two regular bikes. Sarah's and mine, to be exact. Their pedals, chains, and sprockets were hooked to the tandem bike through a common axle, which was no small task of design and mechanics, may I humbly say. I didn't want to count how many skinned knuckles and U clamps and quarter-inch nuts and bolts and lock washers and hours of hacksawing that all took.

"Amazing, really," my father said as he stared at the bike-car.

"Thank you," I said modestly.

The *Princess*, shaped roughly in a triangle, had a cargo bay of four lightweight aluminum lawn recliners bolted on either side of the main frame and secured to a wire-mesh floor. The main supplies—tents, sleeping bags, tools, food, and water—were already packed. If things went totally bust, we could always unload the *Princess* and start a pedicab business.

Straight up from the center of the *Ali Princess* rose my true inspiration: the sixteen-foot wooden mast and sail that had belonged to my father's boat, the *Tonka Miss*. To make the *Princess,* I had cannibalized every piece of sports equipment the Newell family owned.

"Now boarding," I said, trying to sound upbeat. Trying to sound as if we were heading out on a fun-filled family vacation.

"Are you sure she'll carry us all?" my mother asked, hesitating at the *Princess.*

"Yes," I said sharply. My tolerance for annoyance was low these days. Maybe it was the times, maybe it was turning sixteen, maybe it was a combination of the two. I had waited for years to be old enough to get my driver's license, and now that I was sixteen, nobody drove anymore. Some luck. But the *Princess* had nothing to do with luck. I'd built her from top to bottom. There was no way she wouldn't work.

Sarah was up and moving, thanks to my mother. From sitting in the dust in her black clothes, Sarah now had a white butt. Ash on her ass. But my sense of humor had slipped a bit these days, and I didn't say anything. Actually her smudged clothes gave her a black-and-white camouflage look perfect for tonight.

"What do I do now?" Sarah said. At the *Princess* she made like she didn't know where to get on.

Talk about annoying. I'd shown her ten times—minimum—how the *Princess* worked, where to sit, how to pedal.

"Here," I said, hoisting my sister up into the left cargo bay. "Sit here and you won't have to do anything—which is nothing new."

She shot back some remark, which I ignored. With the stiff breeze tonight, we could get by with less than a full crew pedaling. I made sure she was situated. As my parents climbed aboard, I strummed the main guy wires for one last check. Fine lines of rock flour puffed away and shimmered like frost in the air. The wires were as tight as bass-guitar strings. I went down my presail checklist. "Masks?" I asked.

My parents nodded. We tightened our elastic drawstrings behind our heads. Sarah begrudgingly followed suit. The ash was so fine that it was easy to forget about masks. The white surgical-type ovals were free at any hospital, police station, or post office, and most people wore them. Those who were too cool to be seen wearing one in public soon coughed like coal miners on four packs a day.

My mother turned to look back at our house. It was a huge house, way larger than any family needed—big enough for a half dozen families. And it was not our "real" house. That was in south Minneapolis, where I grew up. But after my father made it with the Shawnee Kingston Jazz Band, we moved to the suburbs. He figured that a major house with pool and tennis court would make up for him being on the road all the time. At least that was my theory. But I always felt stupid when my friends, all of whom lived in normal-sized houses, bused out with their skateboards or their tennis racquets so they could play on the Newell family concrete or splash in our pool. My excuse was that my mother had her business (a small literary agency) in our home and she entertained clients a lot. But that was lame. Anyone could see that her business took up only a couple of upstairs rooms. Mostly I liked to visit my friends back in the old neighborhood rather than have them come here to this house that was only a moat and a turret short of a castle. Trouble was, after I visited my old neighborhood and then came back home, I felt strange. Kind of twilight zone. Like living in the suburbs was not real life. Like I was neither wolf nor dog.

But my combination garage and shop I would miss. I've always been a tool type. I've built things, starting with Legos, since I could remember. For Christmas and my birthday my parents bought me tools, and over the years I had built up a workshop that looked like a small hardware store. My toughest part of packing for this trip was choosing which tools to take and which ones to leave hanging lonely in the garage.

"We'll be back," Nat whispered to the silent, hulking house. My sister covered her eyes with her hands. My father stared at the house as if something in his life was ending.

But not me. Nothing was ending for Miles Arthur Newell. I was 5 feet 6 inches tall, 136½ pounds, and still growing. I had blue eyes and buzzed hair under an old Rancid cap, and I was better with tools than all the home-improvement guys on television. No stupid natural disaster was going to cheat me out of anything.

CHAPTER TWO

OVER TWO YEARS EARLIER

THE THREE OF US WERE at the family dinner table. Sarah and my mother had been arguing over Sarah's newly purple hair, and in grim silence my mother passed me the green beans. At that moment from the basement— at least it sounded like it was from there—came a faint *thud*. We all looked at each other. It was as if my father was down there, in his music studio, and had given his bass drum a single tap. But my father was on the road again. Had been for weeks.

"What was that noise?" Nat asked. She cocked her head. It didn't sound again.

From our chairs we glanced about the dining room and through the windows. "Maybe something fell," I said, and took advantage of the moment to slide the beans toward Sarah without taking any myself.

"Is the security system on?" my mother said, turning to me. Before my father left on the new tour, he had a top-of-the-line home security system installed. "So you'll feel better," as he put it.

"Yes, it's on," I said.

"You haven't been fooling with it again, have you, Miles?"

"No," I said, annoyed.

I thought motion-sensor technology was cool, and soon after it was installed, I couldn't resist taking a peek inside the main power unit. Just a few tiny Phillips-head screws was all it took. Trouble was, within four minutes a rent-a-cop car with flashing lights and two security guards inside came speeding up the driveway to the house. I was impressed; the guards were not, nor was my mother.

"Maybe there's someone down there!" Sarah said, her blue eyes widening.

"There's no one in the basement," I said. I made a show of slouching up from my chair and clumping down the long stairs. It was the least I could do for my mother. And, as everyone knows, clumping one's feet is always important when it comes to weird noises in the basement.

The downstairs still felt strange. All my father's musical equipment, including his big trap set with all its drums and cymbals—the stuff I'd grown up with— was missing. The space down here was always too big, but now it looked like an empty gymnasium. I walked around, even rattled open a couple of closet doors. "Dad?" I said softly. There was only silence.

"Nobody there," I announced as I reemerged upstairs. "Told you so."

Sarah let out a huge sigh of relief. Even though she dressed as dark and as scary as she could get by with, she was still a little girl.

"Thank you, Miles," Mother said.

I shrugged. We went on eating.

Later, after dinner, as Sarah and I cleaned up in the kitchen, my mother called our names. Loudly. She was in the den watching the news on television; Sarah and I stared at each other, then hurried in.

"Look!" my mother said. A banner scrolled across the bottom of the screen:

WASHINGTON STATE HAS BEEN ROCKED BY MAJOR VOLCANIC ERUPTIONS. IT IS CONFIRMED THAT ON FEBRUARY 10, 2006, AT 6:13 P.M., MOUNT RAINIER EXPLODED WITH CATACLYSMIC FORCE, WITH A DEATH TOLL IN THE HUNDREDS IN THE TACOMA–SEATTLE AREA. MASSIVE AMOUNTS OF ASH CONTINUE TO SPEW INTO THE AIR. DETAILS TO FOLLOW. . . .

"Those volcano people have been predicting this for months, but I never really thought it would happen!" my mother muttered. She rapidly surfed through the channels. CNN was first on the story, but just barely. The anchorwoman with the long face and big hair was speaking in fragments as she listened to a voice in her earpiece.

"Major seismic event. Massive eruptions. . . . Mount Rainier in Washington State, perhaps Mount Adams as well, plus several small ones in between. . . . Bigger than any of the volcanology forecasts. 'Like a string of firecrackers,'" she continued. "Up to fifty times bigger than Mount Saint Helens."

"Saint who?" I asked.

"Mount Saint Helens," Sarah said immediately. "You know. Washington State?" She didn't include her usual, "If you'd just read for once, Miles." That was her other, younger self. Lately she read only trashy, vampire-type fiction.

"I have friends in Seattle," Nat said softly, as if to herself. "I know people there." She clicked rapidly through the channels. I stood there for a couple of minutes, but no details followed. I'd heard so much—for years, it seemed—about seismic activity in the Cascade Range that it was like old news, like a movie with so much prepublicity and so many television trailers that it feels like you've already seen it. Why go to the theater? I eased toward the front door.

"Miles hasn't filled the dishwasher," Sarah said.

"Fill the dishwasher, Miles," my mother said automatically.

I glared at Sarah and headed back to the kitchen. I was only half finished when my mother called us again. "Children—you really should see this."

I sighed. Sarah hurried off, and I followed at my own pace. On the big-screen Sony a column of ash rose straight up like a gray broccoli stalk, growing even as we watched. Everything below and around it was flat and gray. "My God," my mother murmured. "Mount Rainier really is gone."

Sarah plopped down and leaned her purple head

toward the screen. Close-up images showed a forest tipped over like an exploded box of toothpicks. The scene switched to a suburb of Tacoma. At the edge of the mud slide, cars were washed up in jagged rows like leaves in a gutter after a rainstorm.

Sarah suddenly sucked in her breath and whirled around. "Dad! Where's he playing right now?" I hadn't heard her call him Dad for a long time.

"East Coast. Boston area," my mother said quickly. She touched Sarah's hair. "He's fine. Not to worry."

Sarah brushed off her hand and returned her gaze to the television. There were scenes of crushed houses and rescue workers running around like crazy. It was a first responder's dream come true. That and a great opportunity for documentary filmmakers. I loved those programs with names like *Nature's Fury* and *Savage Earth*. I watched bulldozers carefully uncovering cars. There were people still in them, some alive, some not.

"Do you think we'll have school tomorrow?" I asked.

Both my mother and Sarah turned to stare at me.

"Why wouldn't you have school tomorrow?" my mother asked.

I shrugged. "Just wondering," I mumbled. It was the kind of dumb question that kept getting me in trouble in ninth grade that year. Sarah laughed at me, then turned back to the screen.

"By the way, your purple hair looks stupid," I said.

The next morning in school we were sent to our advisor pods rather than to first-hour class. There, in small groups, we watched continuing coverage of the Cascade Eruption, as it was already being called. All the anchor-people—Joie Chen, Wolf Blitzer, Nancy Rodriguez—were out of their offices and at the scene. But old Dan Rather had them all beat. He was dressed in combat gear—green fatigues, Army helmet against falling pumice stone, goggles, and a major dust mask that made his face look like a grasshopper's head. He breathed heavily, like Darth Vader, as he moved through dust and smoke. Pausing before a leg poking out of the mud, he wheezed, ". . . Vietnam, the Gulf War, I've been there—but nothing compares to this."

We all laughed, except Mr. Worthing and a few science types and Junior Knowledge Bowl geeks who watched the big screen with their mouths hanging open.

Mr. Worthing turned to us. His face looked strange, too white. "I have a cousin who lives—or lived—near Tacoma. We're pretty sure he's dead." And then he turned back to the screen.

The room was quiet. We all looked at each other. Leave it to a teacher to ruin a good time. Nathan Dale Schmidt, a skinny kid with yellow dreds, pushed out his lower lip and made the sign of the cross. We all cracked up, but silently.

"Math question, Miles," Mr. Worthing said without looking.

I can't tell you how I hated the man when he did that.

"Mount Rainier is gone. Vaporized. If it was approximately cone-shaped, with a height of 2.65 miles and a base radius of 6 miles, how much volume would that be?"

I had the usual two options: act dumb and lie, or be smart and look like a geek. The formula popped quickly into my head: $\frac{1}{3} \pi r^2 h$. And if you had the formula, the rest was easy. Sometimes I wished I had recall like normal people. When I was small, at home we played a card game called Memory. Dozens of little animal cards were dealt facedown, and then we took turns drawing two and trying to make pairs. I beat everybody, kids and adults, every time. Memory Boy, my parents called me. . . . Now I scrunched up my face and crunched the numbers. "About a hundred cubic miles, boss," I said.

There were giggles about the room over the "boss" part.

"One hundred cubic miles—and that's just one of the mountains!" Mr. Worthing said. He didn't take his eyes off the screen.

We continued to watch the ash rising from the crater of the former Mount Rainier. Talk about boring. The ash cloud billowed up as gray and repetitious as a screen saver designed by a dropout from Cobol 101. The newscasters hyperventilated over the same stuff: ". . . ash plume will soon reach the stratosphere, about nine to twelve miles above the earth, and begin to disperse into the jet stream," and ". . . possible wide-reaching implication for global weather patterns. . . ."

"Mr. Worthing?" I asked.

"Yes, Miles?"

"Shouldn't we get out of school for this?"

"Why is that, Miles?" Mr. Worthing said without looking.

"I mean, it's a national event of tragic proportions."

"I think our school administration will hold that it's very important to carry on in times like these. Don't you agree, Miles?"

"I'm not sure, sir. At least Mr. Litzke should cancel our

oral-history project." There was a chorus of agreement. The dreaded oral-history project was supposed to start today in social studies. I didn't mind the ninth-grade science project, but I hated anything to do with reading and writing. And in this case, old people.

"We should study volcanoes instead," someone called.

"I'm sure Ms. Guilfoile will be happy to talk about volcanoes in your science class," Mr. Worthing said.

Discussion lagged. The newscasters continued to quack on. There were scenes of bodies being dug up from the mud. I felt some pressure to make a move.

"Mr. Worthing?" I said.

He sighed. "Yes, Miles?"

"Watching this is making me very sad. I'm experiencing feelings of anxiety and grief."

There were snickers.

Mr. Worthing detached his gaze from the screen and slowly turned to me.

I kept a straight face. "I don't think I'm coping well at all, Mr. Worthing. All those dead people. Can I go to the counselor and talk to someone about feeling sad?"

More snickering across the room. Mr. Worthing pursed his lips. I could see he was disappointed in me. Which made me feel terrible. But I couldn't back out now. Once you begin a move, even a stupid one, it's terminal not to follow through.

"Yes, Miles. Of course. If you think you need professional help, then you should have it." There were hoots of laughter—on Mr. Worthing's side this time. He scribbled a pass. "Get out of here," he said. His gaze cut right through me, and then he turned back to the screen and its unending geyser of ash.

I made a triumphant exit, slapping hands here and there. And then I stood outside in the long, empty hallway. For one last laugh I peeked back through the little rectangular window of the classroom. My friends had already turned away.

I watched them for a while, but no one looked my way again, so I plodded along the rows of battered lockers toward the counselor's office. I handed my pass to the secretary. "Hello, Miles!" she said cheerfully. They were always so cheerful here. A couple of losers, one with long hair, the other with a shaved head, stared at me from the battered chairs and couches.

"Hey," I said.

"Hey," they replied, and looked away.

I took a seat and paged through a *Teen Esteem* magazine. The pages were thick and gummy to the touch; all the pictures were defaced. The cheerful, handsome teenagers had poked-out eyes, extra genitals, and rude dialogue boxes added. I sighed. I wondered what was going on back in my advisor pod.

After a while the losers were called inside, and soon Mr. Montroy Jones appeared. "What say, Miles?"

I nodded.

"This way, kid."

I was glad it was him. Mr. Jones was a huge black guy who scared everybody but me. He had once been in prison but then was born again or something. He still had lots of bad tattoos, which he kept to remind him of his "stupid days," as he called them. He was the nicest adult in the school.

He scanned my pass as we entered his office. "Feelings of anxiety and grief over the volcano, Miles?"

I nodded.

He closed the door.

We settled into our chairs.

I tried to put on a sad face. "I have a cousin who might be dead," I said.

He stared at me, then slowly wadded up my pass and made a perfect shot through the tiny basketball net clamped on his wastebasket. "So, Miles. Your old man's still on the road with Shawnee Kingston?"

I shrugged. "Yeah."

"Next time he plays in Minneapolis, you think you can get me tickets?"

I stared.

"Kidding, Miles," he said. "Kidding." He tipped back in his chair and laughed hugely.

I smiled. It was funny. Kind of.

In second-hour science Ms. Audrey Guilfoile was pumped. She was one of those younger teachers who tried to "identify" with her students. I found this annoying, but at least she was lively and always had interesting facts. "The Cascade Eruption is not the first in the world, gang. In fact, dig this." She talked and passed out a sheet. "Way back in A.D. 79 there was the huge eruption of Mount Vesuvius, near Pompeii, Italy— but everybody knows about Vesuvius." As she went on about it nonetheless, I scanned the handout:

Iceland, 1783, Skaptar Jokull volcano. Hundreds of deaths, and the following years 1783–84 were unusually cool. A "dry fog" hung over the land, cutting off incoming sunlight; "rays collected in a burning glass would scarcely kindle brown paper." —Benjamin Franklin.

"This material comes from a great book called *Ring of Fire*, by author David Ritchie," Ms. Guilfoile said. "It's available in the library. Anybody know where the library is?"

There were a few distracted chuckles; most everybody was actually reading.

Indonesia, 1815, Tambora volcano. It sent 36 cubic miles of rock ash into the air. The following year, 1816, became known as "the year without summer." Eastern Canada experienced such a poor harvest that starvation became a significant cause of death among low-income families. France and Britain were plagued by crop failures, and in some parts of Europe the populace was reduced to eating rats, cats, dogs, and anything that would fit into a pot.

"Does this mean we're going to have to eat our pets?" Dara Jamison asked.

There was laughter. She was very weird, always dressed in black and purple—the kind of girl my sister thought was cool.

"This is a volcanic incident, Dara, not a Stephen King novel," Ms. Guilfoile said. "Be sure to tell your dogs and cats and hamsters they're safe."

I read on:

Indonesia, 1883, the Krakatoa eruption. Although it killed thousands . . . the most striking effect had to do with the air. Much of the material blown into the atmosphere by Krakatoa was exceedingly fine. The volcano acted like a giant grindstone during its eruption. Bits of pumice lifted easily into the air and spread around the earth, wafted along by the jet stream. . . . World climate cooled perceptibly all through the late 1880s.

Ms. Guilfoile softly drummed her fingers as the class read. Some students moved their lips and were still on paragraph one. But she couldn't wait. I liked that about her.

"Let's jump ahead to 1980," she said. "Washington State and the Mount Saint Helens eruption—also on the Cascade Range. Its gray cloud turned noon to midnight. Ash the consistency of confectioners' sugar piled up in the streets of Yakima, Washington, and other towns. Some could be bulldozed away, or scraped off rooftops, or shoveled out of the way, but most had to be hosed away. This put severe strain upon water supplies and sewage systems. Several small towns were almost totally buried."

There was silence.

"Aren't bodies totally preserved in the ash?" Dara said.

People groaned.

"She's obsessed with dead bodies," someone called out.

Dara didn't hear. "Like at Pompeii, people can be dug up almost two thousand years later and still have their eyelashes," she added.

There were louder groans.

"Not sure about the eyelashes, Dara," Ms. Guilfoile said easily. "But we'll definitely see the effects of the Cascade blast even here in the Midwest. First, we'll probably start to notice some haze, and more intense sundowns and sunups. Not that any of you have seen a sunrise recently."

There was laughter, and science class rolled on.

Dara whispered to me, "I still think we're going to have to eat our pets."

CHAPTER THREE

ALL ABOARD

THE *ALI PRINCESS* WAS READY. "It's time," I said. With my parents reunited on their bicycle, I gave the *Ali Princess* a push start. She was heavier than I'd hoped for—a lot heavier. However, once moving, the *Princess* rolled easily, and I scrambled into the back bay and took the right rear pedals.

"Hey, this is not hard," my father called over his shoulder as he steered us down the curving cul-de-sac driveway.

"Great," I said evenly. We'd been on the road only ten seconds, plus we were going downhill. But I'd given him the front for a reason: He might feel like he was making some kind of family contribution. For a change.

I had to be in back by the main axle and sprocket in case we had mechanical problems. As well, the whole drive-chain assembly would need occasional oiling. I saw myself like one of those smudged, greasy oiler guys in the bowels of the old steamships where pistons were as big as cars. In the movie *Titanic* the best scenes were of the engine room followed (a very close second) by Leonardo DiCaprio doing his charcoal sketch of Kate Winslet. I'd rewound to both a few times.

But the *Ali Princess* was not the *Titanic*. It was clear sailing ahead, and all parts turned smoothly. White pumice kicked up behind, then exhaled back onto our skinny tire marks and obscured them. Perfect. The less evidence that we had left town, the better.

When I lived in the woods, I never walked the same trail twice. Nobody knew where my cabin was. That's because I never left any tracks. I was as paranoid these days as old Mr. Kurz, my oral-history "buddy" from ninth grade. Twice I had seen footprints in the ash alongside our house and garage, tracks that led back toward the Hofmeyers, our nearest neighbors. We'd been sort of friends with them—parents and the children—for several years, but things were different now. People had passed through a "come-together, help-your-neighbor" mentality and now looked out for number one. Hoarding was against the law, but everybody did it. Nobody thought they had enough food. Everybody worried that their neighbors had more.

The *Ali Princess* rocked briefly side to side.

"Everything okay?" I called to my father.

"Just testing the steering," he said. He glanced back at my mother, who pedaled steadily. "Piece of cake, really."

We rolled on. Houses were all nearly dark. Electricity was rationed and expensive. Most streetlights were shut off as well, which was fine by me. The less attention tonight, the better. We turned onto the empty boulevard, heading east toward the freeway entrance. Any vehicles out after dark would be the cops, ambulance drivers, or truckers. Gasoline supplies were restricted, though available on the black market—especially from farmers. But big deal. Who knew any farmers? And anyway, "nonessential" travel was forbidden. If the cops stopped you for a destination check and found out you were just cruising, your car was confiscated on the spot.

It was not that the country was low on supplies of gas or other forms of energy. Rather, the big power plants were part of the problem. Nuclear generators, oil refineries, coal-burning producers—all were reduced to minimum operating levels in order to keep from further screwing up air quality. And since the biggest contributors to air pollution were automobiles, they were first on the government's air-quality hit list. On the other hand, those empty streets were great for skaters, in-liners, bicyclists—and the *Ali Princess*.

We neared the streetlights of downtown Wayzata. The ever-falling mist of ash swelled their globes into giant round dandelion pods ready to burst with white seed. Below their skinny iron stems, the streets were empty. The Fresh Mart Produce Store marquee read, LETTUCE AND TOMATOES AVAILABLE WEDNESDAY! (CUSTOMER LIMITS). The hardware store, with plywood on its lower windows, read, NO GASOLINE/PROPANE/BOTTLED WATER KEPT HERE OVERNIGHT. Here and there a business was boarded up. Dust drifted and swirled down Main Street, which looked like a ghost town.

I didn't like it. The lights above were too bright, the street below too dim. I kept a sharp eye through the dust-fog and touched my aluminum baseball bat, ready in the cargo bay. I hadn't played baseball since Little League—I quit when I got into skateboarding—but I also had not forgotten what it feels like to get whacked. Big Chris Long struck out one day, and flipped his bat behind him toward the dugout. I was on deck—had my helmet on—but still got knocked cold. I remember hearing the *Whack!* on my head, then seeing bright, floaty things. Now I squeezed my bat's rubber-wrapped neck. Strange how things like bats and hammer handles and golf clubs feel so good in your hands. Like they were made to be swung.

We were just about through town when I heard a noise. A sharp chirp—then another—nails being wrenched from wood. "Look," my mother whispered, and pointed. Through the haze, ahead on the right, four figures in dark clothes with dust rags tied over their faces were prying loose a sheet of plywood from a house that looked abandoned. Nails groaned under their crowbars.

"That's not the Sears home fix-it crew," I whispered. "Keep pedaling."

Sarah, slouched in the luggage bay, sat up and began to look around with alarm. We leaned harder into our pedals, and the wheels purred faster over the pale, floury street. The *Princess* had no squeaks or rattles, and we were almost past when Sarah, the know-everything tough girl, spotted the housebreakers and shrieked.

Just a small screech, but it did the job. The nearest masked man spun around. His head jerked backward as he took in the image of the *Princess*. He pointed, and I heard him grunt something to the others, who turned as well. Suddenly the main (biggest) guy came trotting across the street on an interception course with the *Princess*.

"Oh, damn!" Sarah shouted.

Great. Just great.

"Hey! Hey there!" the man grunted. His voice, muffled by the dust rag, sounded like a bear huffing. He pointed with his crowbar as he ran at us. "Stop. I want to talk to you!"

"Faster!" I hissed to my parents. We leaned into our pedals big time. When we were at top speed, I grabbed the baseball bat and hunkered beside Sarah; she was trying not to look. Crowbar Man kicked up dust as he charged. I read his mind: He would jam his crowbar into the rear wheel spokes and bring us to a crashing halt. It was not a bad plan, but he had not reckoned on a retired Little League catcher who batted over .500 in his golden years.

Things went to slow motion. About two seconds from impact—his crowbar was in range—I went into a batter's crouch and swung. A level swing. Got my hips into it. My bat caught his smaller iron bar just above his fingertips with a sound like a church bell rung by a sledge-hammer. His black bar spun away through the air. The *Princess* slewed briefly sideways from my motion—Sarah herself grabbed my shirt or I might have fallen overboard—but then we regained the straight and narrow. Crowbar Man lay flopping in the street wringing his arm and screaming like he was holding a bare electrical wire and could not let go.

"Next time wear work gloves, loser!" I shouted back. I gave him the one-finger salute, and we sped on. The rest of his gang huffed and puffed into the street, but they were nowhere near as fast as him or us, and soon they disappeared behind in a haze of pale dust.

"That was close," Nat breathed.

"Good work, Miles," my father called. "Couldn't have done it better myself." He tried a laugh, but it went nowhere.

We rolled on, panting and silent. Sarah peeked back wide-eyed. "Are they gone?"

"History," I said.

She turned to me. "Sorry," she said.

I shrugged. "Thanks for grabbing me, by the way," I said.

She managed a small smile.

I touched the sweet spot of my bat. It had a serious dent, which felt good when I touched it, kind of like a scar that had already healed. But scars are memory buttons: Touch them and you get an instant replay. Weirdly, my heart only now started to pound and my armpits to get clammy. I glanced back over my shoulder, but the gang of four was long gone. I let out a breath. Someday it would be nice, again, to be just a slack kid pushing himself around a driveway on his skateboard and doing grinds on the curbs. I felt a little bit like crying. "You all right?" Sarah said.

I managed a nod.

"That was a cool swing," she said.

"Maybe I'll make a comeback in high school baseball."

"You'll be too old for high school," she said, reverting to tough-girl Sarah.

"And you'll have to make all new friends—which wouldn't be a bad thing."

Sarah said something very nasty.

"Sarah! Miles!" my mother said. "No arguing in the car."

We rolled along in comfortable silence. It felt good to be a family of four again.

"And anyway, what are we going to do about school?" Sarah said.

"There are schools up north," my mother replied.

"Probably stupid ones," Sarah said.

"We'll do home school. I'll be your teacher," I said.

"Miles!" my mother said.

"Okay, okay," I replied.

The *Ali Princess* whispered along the empty, ashy streets. My mother kept looking at the dark, dusty suburbs. "This is like a war," she murmured. "People's lives are disrupted, put on hold for a while. Then it ends and we all try to start over again." She looked at my father; he turned to look back at her.

I hoped she was right. I hoped my parents got used to living together again. Maybe they would find out they liked it.

But first things first. "There's our turn," I called to my father.

He steered the *Princess* up onto the entrance ramp of 494, the freeway heading northwest. Below, wind blew steadily up the vacant six-lane channel. It was time to set sail.

CHAPTER FOUR

BACK TO NINTH GRADE

THE FIRST DAY AFTER THE volcano, Mr. Litzke proceeded with our regular social-studies schedule. He wouldn't even talk about the eruption, which none of us wanted to hear more about anyway, but we thought it might throw off the oral-history project. "You'll hear enough about volcanoes in the coming days on the news and in science class."

There was muttering.

"Please take out your oral-history guidelines. Today is an exciting day. We'll be starting our oral-history project with a field trip to Buena Vista nursing home."

There were pained noises. Each student was required
to become "buddies" with a senior at nearby Buena Vista
Convalescent Home. Don't get me started on corny
names in the Midwest that use Spanish words to sound
cool; my Language Loser Award is a motel named Casa
del Toro, which as best as I can figure means "House of
Bull."

Anyway, teachers loved oral history and similar
kinds of "outreach" projects. Cleaning up parks and
riverbanks, building Habitat for Humanity houses
(which I looked forward to next year)—anything to get
us out of the classroom so they didn't have to do any
actual teaching. Anything to put us kids on display so
the Scrooges of the community would vote Yes on the
next school bond issue. Anything to show parents that
the teachers weren't slackers who handed out worksheets
and then kicked back to read the newspaper.

Like Mr. Litzke. Not far from retirement (his hair
had retired long ago), he spent most of each class period
rattling the newspaper and then asking us pop questions
about current events. I got on his bad side one day when
he thought I was volunteering an answer.

"Yes, Miles? You know about the NRA's position
on handguns?" He seemed surprised and pleased

that I had raised my hand.

"No. And how the hell would I? We never get to see the newspaper because you read it all day."

I got detention and a note home, and it was downhill from there. Now, every chance he got, Mr. Litzke stuck it to me.

On this warm February day we bused over to Buena Vista (who would trust ninth graders to walk three blocks?). Outside the home a few old-timers were parked in wheelchairs facing the sun. Some had nodded off. Others sat slumped with their heads slacked to one side or their mouths open. "Not to worry," Mr. Litzke said as we unloaded. He gave me a particularly smug look. "You'll be assigned to someone who can still talk and think and tell all sorts of wonderful stories."

"Stories like how it feels to wear diapers again?" I muttered as we neared the front doors. Under one of the wheelchairs was a shiny little puddle of pee.

Inside, the place had gleaming white long hallways with square corners and curved mirrors above them to prevent wheelchair collisions. The whole place smelled funny, kind of like sourdough bread. Residents moved along in their walkers or wheelchairs; rubber tips and wheels squeaked on the bright floor. They didn't look around much. It was like their brains had been sanitized by breathing fumes from too many antiseptics and cleaning fluids. But the geezers all seemed to be heading down the hall in one direction.

Mr. Litzke met with the administrator, then began to call out our names. An attendant, a male-nurse type guy in white pants, white tennis shoes, and thin ponytail, passed out name tags. Mine read Hans Kurz.

"Han Solo?" Nathan Schmidt whispered to me.

The administrator, a middle-aged guy in a skinny tie, said, "Welcome to Buena Vista. Each of you now has the name of your new friend. They're all assembled in the Rec Room, waiting for you, so why don't we head down there too?"

In the Rec Room the old-timers were lined up in wheelchairs, or else leaned on walkers, or else slumped in folding chairs. They each wore a large name tag with a first name and last initial of someone in our class.

"Please step forward and introduce yourself," Mr. Litzke called.

We reluctantly began to move up and down the row of geezers. Soon everybody found his or her "buddy." Everybody except me. I looked around. While I didn't particularly want a "buddy," neither did I want to be standing there like a loser. Everyone stared at me.

"Ha, ha, Miles!" Nathan whispered.

The administrator checked his clipboard, then turned to the male nurse in white pants and white tennis shoes. "Where's Mr. Kurz?"

The nurse grinned slightly. "Wouldn't come. Says he hates kids."

Everybody in the class laughed. At me. I wasn't bothered in the least. I thought the nurse was cool—possibly an adult troublemaker. And I thought I might even like Mr. Kurz. Anybody who hated ninth graders couldn't be all bad.

"So what's your name, kid?" the male nurse said as we walked down the hall toward Mr. Kurz's room.

"Miles. Miles Newell."

"Miles, this is your lucky day." He chuckled.

We stopped at door 29A and tried to push it open. It was barricaded from the inside.

The nurse rapped sharply, then put his ear to the wood. "Mr. Kurz?"

"Go away!" came a raspy voice.

"Mr. Kurz? Hans? Move away from the door, please."

"I am away from the door, damnit. I'm trying to watch the news."

"But you must have accidentally put something against the door. It feels blocked." The nurse winked at me.

"Hee, hee!" came a hoarse laugh.

"Got a visitor for you," said the male nurse. "A friend wants to see you."

There was silence.

I made pantomime motions that I really didn't need to see him. That I was running late, had a taxicab, a plane to catch, those sorts of motions.

"You can't fool me," Mr. Kurz said. "I never had any friends. I always lived alone."

"It's never too late to make a friend," the nurse said, all the while pushing against the door, and beginning to make some progress.

"I'm ninety years old. I don't need any friends," rasped the voice.

The nurse pulled me in after him.

A very old man with a leathery face sat in bed with a sheet pulled up to his waist. He was fully dressed, including a heavy wool plaid shirt; and we could see the outlines of boots on his feet. But I couldn't take my eyes off his eyebrows; they were as thick as squirrel tails. White hairs stuck out all over the place. I had never seen eyebrows that bushy.

"What I need is some peace and quiet," the old man growled. His eyes went back to the overhead television.

"Mr. Kurz," the nurse said, "meet Miles Newell. Miles, Mr. Kurz."

Mr. Kurz glanced at me briefly, then turned back to the screen.

"Congratulations," the nurse said to me on his way out. "You guys are now officially 'buddies.'" The door latched behind him.

I sat there as Mr. Kurz watched volcano coverage. I yawned. Several minutes passed. Suddenly the old man began to laugh, a hoarse, wheezing laugh that went on and on.

"Excuse me? Sir?" I finally asked.

He hawked into a paper cup, then turned to me. "Hard times gonna come again, boy."

"Hard times?" I asked.

He nodded. "Like the Great Depression, only worse. This time it will be dog eat dog. Root hog or die."

I thought of Dara Jamison.

"And you know why, kid?" His blue eyes bored into mine.

"Ah, no sir."

He wheezed out another long laugh. "Because people don't know how to do anything anymore. Oh, they're good with computers and all those electronic gadgets. But they forgot the old ways."

"The old ways?"

"How to make it on your own if you have to. How to find food, stay warm, live off the land," he rasped. "Let them eat their e-mail. Let them burn their computers to stay warm at night—then they'll find out. Don't you see?" He laughed so hard, he hunched over in a coughing fit.

"I see," I answered. I saw that Mr. Litzke had really stuck it to me this time.

ADIÓS

WITH THE *ALI PRINCESS* PAUSED at the top of the
freeway, we looked back at the city. To the east was
the faint, gloomy outline of downtown Minneapolis.
The skyscrapers were dark giant statues carved in iron.
Below, the carless freeway was an empty river with a
windswept concrete floor.

"I need you to run the sail," I said to my father. I
glanced at my mother.

My father kept looking at the ghostly city skyline. I
wondered if he was thinking of jazz concerts he had
played; of the other musicians in the Shawnee Kingston

band. Sometimes I thought they were his real family.

"Me?" he said suddenly.

"Sure," I answered.

He shrugged. "I'll give it a try."

Nat was silent; she watched him. He crawled to the rear of the *Princess* and looked at the ropes, the fabric rolled around the boom. "How does this thing work?" he asked.

"Just like a sailboat. Same as the old *Tonka Miss*—only with wheels."

"No sweat." As he loosened the tie-down cords, he automatically turned his face to catch the breeze, test its angle. That was a good sign.

I went up front and took the handlebars; I would steer us.

"Ready?" he asked.

I gave him a thumbs-up.

"Now departing, pier seven," I called. Nobody laughed.

My father used to be a good sailor. In one motion he ran up the fabric—its little rings jangled against the cable—and swung the boom sideways. Fabric caught the wind with a sharp *ca-shuck!* sound. Air punched open the sail.

The *Princess* lurched forward. "Whoa!" my father exclaimed. He struggled against the rope.

Momentarily the *Princess* heaved up on her front tire.

"Spill some air!" I shouted.

My father dumped half the wind just before we tipped. Then the *Princess* righted herself with a jolt and swept down the ramp into the concrete valley. Everybody screamed as if we were on a roller coaster at the state fair. Within seconds we were going close to thirty miles per hour. I clutched the handlebars like death, but the *Princess* ran straight and true—just like I knew she would. Once onto the freeway, I let out a breath.

My father, wedged in the left rear bay, worked the boom from a single rope around his forearm. The wind was perfect. He leaned outward partway to counterbalance the wind, and for an instant I flashed back to the good old days, before the ash. My father had a real job then—he was a high school music teacher— and was home weekends like other dads.

We would sail all day on Lake Minnetonka, from island to island, angling around bays, tacking back and forth. When I was really small, about four or five years old, it hit me one day that we had sailed clear across the lake with a strong wind straight against us. I thought this was a miracle—that my father could sail against the wind by going sideways. And it was clear to me then that dads were for just that: miracles. It was one of the happiest moments of my life.

"Miles! Look out!" my mother called. She pointed suddenly at an upcoming freeway overpass. "The mast—it's not going to clear the—"

"Overpass?" I finished, as we sped underneath. I didn't even look up; I had done my road research. I knew every bridge and its height from here to Birch Bay. "Standard freeway construction. A foot to spare and then some," I called out. We skimmed along leaving a silent, tumbling wake of pumice-like waves on moonlit water.

"Wow," Sarah said to me. She couldn't help herself; she was actually impressed.

Here and there along the vacant freeway, abandoned cars lay like roadkill. Wheels and hoods were ripped off; doors were gone, eaten away by scavengers. Beyond the skeleton hulks of cars, under the bridges and in the shrubbery on the side slopes of the banks, were tiny red eyes of campfires. They were not big blazes, but more like embers—little secret fires among the bushes where the dark shapes of homeless people lay.

Homeless people: That was us—but not quite. At least we had someplace safe to go to.

Directly ahead, at pavement level, two men leaned against a concrete bridge column and passed a bottle. One of them took a long drink under his dust rag, his eyes closed as we sailed past. The other one jerked backward in surprise as we whooshed by; he began to wave an arm and point after us and jabber at his companion, but by the time the other man looked, we were long gone. Like frosty breath on a winter night.

But it was summer, July 5, and warm for a change. We sailed on. I commanded the handlebars and my father the sail. The dark suburbs unwound behind us in a steady but thinning stream.

Deep into the night, near three A.M., I was sleepy at the wheel until I saw, closing from the north, a Romulan attack vessel. I jerked fully alert, but the hallucination kept coming. It had a massive, pointed iron mask and running lights that swept side to side and low to the ground. From the heavy rumble I realized that it was a truck.

Not just one truck: it was the leader of a convoy coming into the city. A huge steel nose, half battering ram and half plow, jutted up front. Iron wings rode just off the concrete, and sparked down at times like an electric welder with irregular power. All that iron was to knock away debris or roadblocks thrown up by bandits. The trucks also wore metal wheel skirts that reached nearly to the pavement, these to prevent anyone from shooting out the tires. The lead truck swung a spotlight on us, and I could see the glint of a gun barrel in its light. But we were breaking no law, and the convoy rumbled on in a tumbling whirlwind of dust. Maybe its drivers thought the *Ali Princess* was a hallucination.

Along about four in the morning we reached open fields. The wind blew stronger and steadier here, and the *Princess* picked up speed. My mother (I made sure she was strapped in) was asleep in the cargo bay; Sarah was a dark lump of luggage. The freeway ran straight north now, and my father had to hold the boom hard to the right side in the stronger wind. The wheels hissed and kicked up dust like a garden hose spraying whitewater. To keep his balance and get maximum wind, my father hung out horizontally—barely inches above the pavement. I caught my breath; concrete was not water, and he should at least be wearing a helmet and skateboarding elbows. But then again, he was doing fine. The image of him hanging out there was better than any photo I'd seen in any of his old sailing magazines. I wished that my mother and Sarah were awake to see him. I wished that I could just tell him how cool he looked right now, but I had all I could do to keep the front wheel steady.

Toward dawn the wind faded as if chased by the light. The gray sky leaked blue, then yellow, then pink, then an orange that looked fluorescent, or else like a huge cone of molten lava pushing up from the fields and trees. Then the big moment: the rim of the sun broke above the horizon line like a giant asteroid rising, not falling—and when it hit the giant, pale lake of the sky, ripples of intense color spread in slow-motion waves. Like rainbows, the extra color at sunrise and sunset had a scientific explanation. Sulfur dioxide, the main gas emitted by the volcanoes, combined with oxygen and water to form sulfuric acid gas, which then condensed into fine droplets, or aerosols, which then hung in the air and made haze. Still, it was damn beautiful.

"Huh? What?" Sarah said with alarm. She started awake, blinking, confused; then her eyes widened as she saw the sunrise.

"Pretty, yes?" I said softly.

"Wow," she murmured in her little-girl voice.

My mother was stirring too. She smiled at the sunrise,

then turned quickly to me. "You want me to take the driver's seat for a while? I could steer."

My fingers ached from clenching the wheel, and I suddenly was tired in a major way. "Sure," I answered. Carefully, by inching along on opposite sides of the main frame, we changed positions. In the rear, my father remained at his post. He was ghostly gray from dust, an ancient sailor from another time.

"You need a break, Dad?" I asked him.

"No, I'm good. The wind's flattening out. Doesn't take so much work now."

Our speed had dropped considerably, but we still rolled along at a good leg-kick, skateboarding pace. "Why don't you get some shut-eye, Miles?" he said. His voice sounded momentarily like it used to. In the good old days.

I didn't have to be asked twice. Sarah, without complaint, actually took a bicycle seat so I could stretch out in the luggage bay. My mother's little wireless television/radio came on at low volume. Like most adults, she obsessed on the news—especially nowadays. News was like a drug for adults. They had to have it. But what good did it do? Especially when it was all bad. Luckily the whirring pavement beneath me muted the radio's sound, and as the concrete rushed on in a never-ending stream, I felt my eyelids drooping.

I woke to the sound of panting. The light was brighter now, a brilliant dry fog that stung my eyeballs. For a second I didn't know where I was.

"Wind's shifted," my father said.

"This is hard," Sarah groaned, pedaling and making a big show of being totally exhausted. I took a moment to savor the sight of my sister actually doing some work, then fished out my map.

"We're just north of Little Falls. We're on Highway 10 now," my mother said.

"How much longer do we have to pedal?" Sarah asked.

The answer was a sudden *slap-whacka, whacka!*

"Chain off!" I said, springing into action. "Pull over. Nice and slow."

My father spilled the sail as my mother steered us neatly onto the shoulder. When we'd stopped, they glanced at each other: It must have been a marriage moment, as I called them—something about working together.

"Good, because I have to pee anyway, plus I'm hungry," Sarah said.

"You kids' timing was always amazing," my mother replied. She looked ahead up the highway to a cluster of buildings including a tall golden arches sign. "On our trips up north you always woke up about here—just before we stopped for gas and McDonald's."

"It's probably closed and boarded up—like everything else," Sarah said, looking toward the far-off yellow arches.

We climbed off and slapped dust from our clothes. There was a grove of short, shaggy pine trees, someone's Christmas tree plantation, just off the expressway. *My cabin was deep in the pines. I didn't want anybody sneaking up on me. I kept all my important stuff hidden. You can't trust nobody these days.*

"Let's push the *Princess* in here, out of sight, then walk," I said.

After we secured the *Princess* out of sight, which necessitated dropping the mast, we waited as my mother put on "the vest." It was a backpack sewn under a smock, from when she had us kids. Now the maternity blouse held all our money, papers, shot records, etc. As my mother shifted it over her belly, Sarah rolled her eyes (she thought it was embarrassing). My father thought it was funny. I thought it was clever, even brave of her. With the vest in place, she looked perfectly, naturally, pregnant.

"Nothing, not a word from anyone," she warned us.

"Did we say anything?" I asked.

"No, but you were about to."

We trudged along the shoulder toward the golden arches. In the parking lot were several farm tractors, dust free, plus a convoy of six tractor trailers.

"Here we are," my mother said, "back to civilization. So to speak."

We quickened our pace. I was hungry too.

As we approached the parking lot, a large man with a shaved head and a tattered NWO T-shirt swung out of the nearest cab and stood on the running board. Clearly an unemployed pro wrestler, now he carried a major-looking assault rifle.

"Good morning!" my mother said cheerfully.

"It's just us, the Swiss Family Robinson," Sarah said softly. I have to admit that, on rare occasions, she has a sense of humor. And she's really not dumb, just pathetic most of the time.

"Do not approach the trucks," the guard said,

stiffening his back. He wore mirrored sunglasses. What a cliché, I thought. But that rifle was impressive.

"Just heading to the restaurant," my mother said pleasantly. "It is open, yes?"

"Why wouldn't it be?" the guard growled.

My mother flashed him a smile. "Have a great day," she said. Under her breath she added, "That guy has clearly taken too many body slams."

Inside, the place was full of farmer types and businessmen. There was a major pause as they gave us the twice-over. We smiled. My mother waddled to the counter. Slowly their conversation resumed, but I kept looking around. It was odd to see a full restaurant of people drinking coffee and eating eggs and pancakes like it was back in the 1990s.

"Order me a number three, okay?" Sarah said as she headed to the bathroom. Several men followed her with their eyes. Behind the counter the greaseheads wore the usual short-sleeved stupid uniforms with shiny name tags that said SHERRI and JUSTIN and DAVE—ASST. MANAGER. Everybody had the usual perky smiles. Above the counter were the usual mug shots of burgers and drinks, though I noticed that the prices were blank.

"Maybe the sky's not falling after all," my mother said to my father as she looked around the place.

He said something back that made her laugh.

My parents (probably all parents) have coded language they've developed, and I can usually interpret it, but today I was too hungry to bother. It was just nice to see them together, talking. When we finished ordering, the cashier (Sherri) looked up brightly and said to my mother, "That will be ninety-two fifty."

"Excuse me?" my mother asked.

The clerk repeated the price.

"Are you kidding?" My mother laughed. "Almost a hundred bucks for breakfast at McDonald's?"

The clerk shrugged. Her smile slipped, and conversation died as people turned to stare.

My mother glanced about at the full restaurant, then back to the clerk. "So tell me, is everyone in this town rich? How do all these people afford such prices?"

"Well, actually they don't," Sherri murmured.

"What do you mean?"

"Ah, they live here."

There was absolute silence in the restaurant. Sherri looked behind for help.

"Just pay," I whispered to my mother.

"You mean you have two sets of prices?" my mother pressed.

Dave the Assistant Manager stepped forward. "That's right, folks. One for local people. One for strangers."

At the word *strangers*, the silence got even quieter.

"Miles is right," my father said softly to my mother. "Just pay, and we'll be on our way."

My mother bit her lower lip and slapped down five twenty-dollar bills.

"Here or to go?" the clerk asked. Her cheerful face was back.

"Here!" my mother said. "If we're going to pay over ninety dollars for breakfast, at least we deserve a damn table."

We ate, and made sure we used plenty of syrup and catsup. My mother continued to fume over the prices, but the rest of us ate. And ate. It was like we'd never had fast food before. We were sweaty by the time we finished pancakes and eggs, juice and milk and coffees. A man in the next booth watched us eat. He had a kindly, round face and a seed-corn cap tilted to one side.

"You folks must have been hungry." He smiled.

"You got that right," my mother said.

"Passing through?"

"That's right," she answered.

"That's good," he said; his kindly smile slipped a bit.

My mother raised one dark eyebrow; she didn't reply.

"What I mean is, we got more and more people think they got to get out of the cities," the man said. "They think if they get themselves to a small town, other people will take care of them." Men around him nodded.

"Nope, that wouldn't be us," my mother said, her voice picking up the edges of his speech, finding his own rhythms and bouncing them back. "We're headed north . . . on vacation. Right, gang?"

We all nodded pleasantly, then bent low to wipe our mouths.

Outside, my father let out a long breath.

"That was scary," Sarah said, looking over her shoulder.

"We'd best keep moving," my father said, looking up at the sky. The light was grayer now, and the air felt cooler. I looked over my shoulder and saw white, round faces staring at us through the windows of McDonald's. The truck convoy guard stood motionless as we passed. I could feel his eyeballs moving sideways behind his mirrors.

Back at the pine plantation I took some time to get

the chain back on and inspect the running gear. I didn't like the way the pumice had worn down the teeth on the main sprocket. The sharp points were rounded off a full eighth inch. I considered oiling the chain but decided against it; the oil was picking up grit, and the grit was grinding down the metal points. I had two spare chains and a spare sprocket, but still, the amount of wear worried me.

"Everything okay, motorhead?" Sarah asked. It was her way of apologizing for being occasionally pathetic. There was a chance she might turn into a decent teenager someday.

"Ten four. We're good to go." I hoisted the mainmast and locked it in place.

"Maybe in a previous life you were a trucker," Sarah said.

"Or a sailor," my father said.

"Mechanic, I think," my mother added.

It was their way of thanking me, and under my dust mask I smiled.

"The wind is switching to the northwest," my father said. "Cold front coming in." My father knew his weather; that always impressed me.

"Which means?" my mother said. After stashing the

vest, she was back to her regular slim shape.

"Just like sailing. Means we may have to hunker in for a while somewhere and wait it out," he said.

"But not here," Sarah answered, looking over her shoulder toward the McDonald's. "It's way too creepy."

"Up the road a ways. The Mississippi should be just ahead," I said.

We pedaled briskly past the exit ramp and didn't look back. My father tried to tack left and right against the wind, but the freeway was not wide enough to make the angling effective. Pedaling was harder and harder.

"It feels like we're going uphill," Sarah panted.

"We are, slightly," I said. "We're following the river, which flows south. In fact there's almost five hundred feet of elevation drop from the headwaters to Minneapolis."

"Ask Mr. Science," Sarah said.

"Hey, I've done my homework—what have you done?"

"Children, children," my mother said.

"It's the syrup," my father said to her. "The post-McDonald's sugar burst, remember?" He looked at her.

"All too well!" she said. I could tell that she was smiling underneath her dust mask.

A couple miles north of the interchange, where the highway angles northwest, the wind turned full against us.

"Let's pull in up ahead, by the river," I called.

Nobody argued. When we stopped, I lowered her mast, and then we rolled the *Princess* off the road and carefully down by the bridge and the river. We lay on the dusty, grassy slope and got our breath. Above us, swallows fluttered and dipped through the bridge supports, annoyed at our presence. They had little mud nests tucked up under the massive concrete forms.

"So, here we are," Sarah began.

"Good progress for day one," I said.

Nobody said anything.

"How long we gonna be here?" Sarah said, looking up at the dark concrete roof.

"For a while. Until the wind shifts," I said.

"So what do we do while we're here?" Sarah asked.

"Whatever," I said.

My father lay fully back and closed his eyes. Soon my parents were dozing and Sarah was reading. I checked the map. We were way more than halfway: at least ninety miles away from home, and fifty or less miles to go.

Birch Bay, that was our name for it. A log cabin on

Gull Lake. It had belonged to my grandparents, whom I never knew, and was surrounded by birch and pine trees. We went there every summer for several weeks when my father was a teacher. In the last few years, however, we had made it up there only a couple of weekends during the summer. Birch Bay was one of the reasons I had wanted to get my driver's license: so I could drive up to the cabin myself. There was an old garage with ancient tools—wood saws and planes and rasps and cutting chisels—and every summer I made a different little wooden boat. The cabin itself had a fieldstone fireplace and bunk beds in the loft. I loved it there. I even didn't mind taking naps—as long as I could sleep outside on the big screened porch. Birch Bay always felt like the safest place in the world.

Unlike this gloomy spot under the freeway bridge. It was damp and smelled odd. Even the Mississippi River was siltier than I expected—as if somebody not far upstream was rinsing a huge brush full of white latex paint. Still, there weren't so many dead fish drifting along now, not like in Minneapolis. Even as I thought that, I saw movement in the shallows. A carp nosed around the rocks, kissing them with his rubbery lips. He was sucking at algae of some kind. I stooped low and tried to get closer for a better look—but he saw me and made a bee line (a fish line?) toward deep water.

"Ha, ha," Sarah said, watching me.

I sat down on a rock and flicked little pebbles into the water.

After a while Sarah said, "You know, it's weird."

"What's weird?" I said without looking up.

"I'm reading this novel, but it's like our lives are suddenly way stranger than fiction."

I looked up. I shrugged. We were silent.

"When we get to Birch Bay, we'll be fine," I said.

She didn't reply.

"I think we've got plenty of money," I said softly, glancing at my parents. "Even the way food costs, we'll be okay."

"And if the money runs out?" she said. Her voice was suddenly not so tough.

"We'll eat fish," I said, pointing. The big old carp had eased back to the shallows just upstream; his dorsal fin poked out of the water and sent out ripples as he nuzzled the mossy rocks. "I'm going to see if I can sneak up on him."

"Don't hurt him!" Sarah said.

I let out an annoyed sound and took three or four

steps closer. I was about to take another when the mortar round landed. A skipping, black-and-white mortar round that landed—*PASHOOM*—directly on the carp. Sarah shouted; I stumbled back, almost twisting my ankle; my parents jerked upright.

A huge eagle had snatched the carp.

"My God!" my mother cried.

Water sprayed as the eagle fanned its wings. It had come in low and hard, its yellow talons outstretched like spears. The carp twisted and flopped wildly in the eagle's clutches, but he was a goner. The eagle tilted sideways and flapped its wide wings low over the water, the carp skipping and slapping along the surface, as the eagle slowly gained altitude.

"Amazing!" my father said as the eagle receded.

"Poor fish," my mother said as she watched him disappear.

I could see that we had a ways to go before we became a hunting-and-gathering family.

As everybody relaxed again, I couldn't. My mother turned on her little television, and I began to poke around the campsite. There was something about it I didn't like. Maybe it was the signs of previous campers: broken glass, some McDonald's wrappers, the remains of a campfire that had blackened the concrete overhead. One area smelled bad; in the rocks was a smudgy white flower of toilet paper. Gross. Camping here was too predictable. I didn't like being this close to the freeway, plus anyone moving on or along the river would spot the *Princess* right away.

Nobody knew where I lived, not even that game warden. I used a different trail every time. In winter sometimes I wore my snowshoes backward. You can't trust anybody these days.

"Turn down that stupid TV, will you?" I said to my mother.

She looked surprised, but obeyed.

I thought of the carp. The lesson here was not to splash around with your fin out of the water.

CHAPTER SIX

BUENA VISTA ON THAT FIRST DAY

"SO WHAT DO YOU WANT from me, anyway?" Mr. Kurz growled.

"I have this assignment to do for ninth-grade social studies," I began.

"Speak up," he said. "You're mumbling."

I cleared my throat. "It's called an oral-history project?"

He looked at me blankly.

"Basically it means we're supposed to talk."

He was silent.

"Then I write down any stories you'd care to tell."

He narrowed his eyes suspiciously. "Stories?"

"Yes. Anything about your life."

He drew back; his big white eyebrows rose and fell. "You don't work for the government?"

I stared. "I'm in ninth grade."

"That don't matter. The government's got spies of every kind. Every age. You can't trust anyone."

"Okay then," I said softly.

He hoisted himself out of bed. He was fully dressed in a red plaid shirt, wool pants, and boots—high, well-oiled leather lace-ups that had seen some miles. It was like he was going hunting or hiking. He tottered over to an armchair by the window. The view was of the gray concrete wall of another wing of the rest home. Buena Vista . . . right.

"What direction is the wind today?" he asked suddenly.

"The wind? Ah . . . I don't know."

"A man should always know which way the wind blows," he said. He tried to peer around the concrete corner of the building. "You can never tell here, 'cause you can't see the leaves move."

Mr. Kurz sank into his armchair, its back turned to me, and pulled a blanket over his legs. He picked up a paperback from a tall pile beside his chair and began reading. I looked closer at the books; they were all outdoor adventure and cowboy novels, many by Louis L'Amour. Mr. Kurz's lips moved as he read.

Thought number one: Go see Litzke and get assigned a different geezer. But that would be humiliating. Thought number two: Hang out here, work on my own stuff, and make up the oral-history report. I was creative. I could patch something together for Litzke. Why not?

"So I'll just sit for a while, if you don't mind," I said.

Mr. Kurz had no reply.

From my backpack I took out skateboard trucks and wheel assemblies that I'd just bought, on the cheap, from Ethan Farrell and Dante Billings, who were always getting new gear. I loved used skate stuff. I built excellent boards out of totally trashed equipment. There was nothing wrong with these particular wheel assemblies except for their bearings. One wheel turned hard, and the other had a rattle in it—but no big deal. Replace two sets of bearings at three bucks each, bolt on the tracks, and I had myself a totally rehabbed board.

From the bottom of my pack I fished out my little socket set, plus an adjustable wrench, and went to work.

In the middle of things a wheel slipped from my

hand; *tacka, tacka-tacka* it went across the shiny hard floor—right toward Mr. Kurz's chair. He dropped his book, snaked down his arm, and snared the wheel before it stopped rolling. He held it up to the light close to his eyes.

"What's this?"

"Ah, it's a wheel."

"I can see it's a wheel."

"Off my skateboard," I said.

He turned. His eyes squinted at the chair, where I'd spread out my tools, the bearings, the races. He raised one big white squirrel eyebrow at me. "What's a skateboard?"

I stared.

Mr. Kurz continued to wait for my answer.

"It's, well, this little board with four wheels."

Mr. Kurz shrugged. "Go on," he said.

I tried. Strangely, it was hard to describe.

"Draw me a picture," Mr. Kurz said. He pointed to his bedstand, where there was paper and pencil.

I drew and he leaned in to look. He smelled kind of like leaves or wood, but it was not a bad smell.

"What do you use it for?" he asked.

"A lot of kids use it for getting around," I answered.

I explained how to roll and kick, roll and kick.

"That's a good invention," Mr. Kurz said, nodding at my drawing. "It doesn't need gas or electricity. And anybody could fix one."

I laughed. "Well, not anybody," I said. I explained to him that I did most of the work on my friends' boards.

"What'd I tell you?" Mr. Kurz said, narrowing his eyes again. "Nobody knows how to do anything anymore."

He fell silent. I went back to work.

"Wrong way—you'll strip the threads," he said. I looked up quickly; I'd thought he was dozing.

He reached out and held the truck steady while I cranked counterclockwise this time. The bearings came out; I showed them to him. He seemed to approve, and we worked on in silence.

I wished I had known my grandparents. Sometimes up at Birch Bay I could feel their presence. I vaguely remember their smells from when I was very young. But that was about all.

"When the ice broke that day, I went through up to my armpits," Mr. Kurz said.

I blinked. I looked up from my work.

Mr. Kurz nodded for me to keep working.

"You see, my mistake was trapping beaver too close

to their house. From all their swimming around, the ice was thin. There's all kinds of ways to die, and I thought I was a goner."

"So what'd you do?" I asked.

"Sometimes even a little bit of preparation will save your life. In my pockets I had a couple of stabbers."

"Stabbers?" I asked.

"Like ice picks, only smaller. Take a good-sized nail, sixteen penny or better, and drive it into a short stub of wood. A hand's length of oak branch is best. Then sharpen the head end of the nail to a fine point. Bingo—you got an ice pick. You should always carry a couple in winter," he said.

"Right," I said. And get permanently expelled from school.

His eyes went dull, like a computer screen going to energy-saver mode, and he leaned back in his chair. Now I really thought he had fallen asleep.

"The ice picks?" I said loudly.

"Yes," he said, blinking. "So I rolled over and hung on to the edge of the ice and thought about things. You can't panic. Even when you're in big trouble, you have to think about things. The water wasn't all that deep. I could feel the bottom. But it was soft and mucky—loon shit I call it—so I couldn't push off from it and get out that way. And I couldn't get a grip on the ice. Then I remembered my picks. I fished them out of my pockets, took one in each hand, then used them to gouge the ice. Get a grip on it. I reached forward as far as I could, dug in with the nails. Little bit at a time, I pulled myself out—something you can't do with just your hands because there's nothing to grab on to."

"So you got out."

"Yes. But I was still in trouble. That day it was thirty below zero."

"So you had to build a fire," I said evenly. My eyes flickered to the stack of worn paperbacks by his chair. I was sure I'd find Jack London's name.

"And fast," Mr. Kurz said. "Trouble was, I couldn't walk. My pant legs had frozen hard as stovepipes. Try walking without bending your knees. I had to drag myself to shore, where there was a dead tree. One the beavers had cut."

How convenient. On the other hand, I knew from Birch Bay that beavers were stupid, and sometimes their trees fell not in the water but on land.

"Lucky I had my hunting knife and some matches."

"Weren't the matches wet?"

"No. They were waxed," he said. "Take stick matches and hold them under a dripping candle. The wax seals the heads against moisture, plus burns real nice once you strike it. Didn't take me long before I had a roaring blaze going. Even got home before dark. I tell you, my cabin looked mighty fine. . . ." Then Mr. Kurz's chin tipped down and he was snoring.

The door opened suddenly and the nurse came in. I thought for a second it was Litzke and tried to sweep my little tools into my backpack, but the nurse didn't care. He adjusted the blanket over Mr. Kurz's legs, then turned to leave.

"Excuse me?" I said.

He paused.

I lowered my voice. "What do you know about Mr. Kurz? Where he came from, that sort of thing?"

"Not much," the nurse said. "All I know is that his family checked him in here last year and hasn't been back."

I glanced at Mr. Kurz, who breathed heavily. "He seems into wilderness and outdoor-survival stuff."

"For sure," the nurse said.

"Did he, like, live in the woods or something?"

The nurse smiled at me. He glanced down at the

adventure novels. "Your guess is as good as mine, kid." Then he checked his wristwatch and moved on.

A bell dinged, which also meant it was time for me to go. As I gathered up my stuff, Mr. Kurz sat up as if his battery had been recharged.

"So, Miles," he said. "Why make ice picks with wooden handles?" His blue eyes bored into mine.

I blinked. I thought about it for several seconds. "I don't know."

"Because if you drop them, they float," he said. "Otherwise, you're dead."

I smiled.

He might have smiled, too, though his face was so wrinkled it was hard to tell.

"I'm supposed to come again next week," I said.

"Suit yourself," Mr. Kurz said, and turned away toward his window.

BROAD DAYLIGHT

BACK BY THE MISSISSIPPI BRIDGE my parents were dozing. I said to Sarah, "I'm going upstream a ways."

"Why?"

"To look for a different campsite."

"What's wrong with this one? At least it has a roof."

I glanced up at the gloomy concrete. "Yeah, but there's just something about this place . . ."

She shrugged and was silent. She watched me go.

I followed the riverbank a hundred yards or so along a narrow animal path that paralleled the water. There were deer tracks in the dust, plus others I couldn't identify. *Trails. Follow the game trails. They'll show you the way. Look around and use what the woods gives you. If you listen, it will tell you what to do. . . .*

I thought about getting my little bottle, the one with Mr. Kurz's name on it, and launching it here in the Mississippi. But it seemed too close to the freeway, and besides, my plan was to do it as we crossed the Mississippi near Birch Bay. It was nicer there.

I kept moving along the trail. Gradually the brush and undergrowth became too thick. I followed the deer tracks as they angled up the bank, and suddenly broke out into a field. From its far-off center, the long rusty finger of an irrigator pipe reached out nearly to the riverbank. This was a central-pivot rig: Stilts on wheels, set at regular intervals, held the pipe several feet off the ground, and little electrical motors on the wheels swung the irrigator slowly full circle about the field. I remembered, when I was a kid, seeing this very sprayer in action. The mists from its water shone in the sunlight and drifted across the highway in little rainbows.

But now the pipe was drooped and rusted. Wild vines from the riverbank had crept into the field and up its stilt legs and wrapped themselves in delicate green loops around the iron struts. Still, it was impressive old technology. I examined the big drive chains that moved the wheels. The electrical cord was frayed and mouse chewed. There was nothing I could use. I was always on the lookout for spare parts, especially metal. My dream was to have my own welder someday. It was the one power tool that my parents wouldn't allow, which only made me want it more. For graduation some kids wanted Corvettes, others wanted Cancún vacations, but I wanted a 220-amp Sears welder with hood. Oh, the stuff I could make . . .

I kept moving along the edge of the field. There were several possible camping spots here, small dusty groves of trees and bushes untouched by anyone. Anywhere but that pissy cave under the freeway.

By suppertime we had our tents up not far from the irrigator pipe. The *Princess* blended in perfectly behind the stilt wheels and pipes. Our tracks were already covered by wind-blown ash; any that remained, I brushed away with a branch full of dried leaves.

My mother fixed us a major pouch dinner (add boiling water and seal) of chicken and rice. There was camper's cheesecake for dessert. Then we headed to our tents before it got dark. My parents had to share one, and Sarah and I had a smaller dome. She and I hated this arrangement, but what could we do? "Do you mind, like, leaving while I get my pajamas on?" she asked.

I let out an exasperated breath. First, who changes into pajamas when you're camping? And second, it wasn't like I wanted to see anything. I took a hike.

Down by the river I poked along the shore and looked for stuff and tossed an occasional rock into the water. I planned to stay clear until Sarah was asleep so we wouldn't have to speak to each other. I pitched a stone as far as I could. It went out of sight in the gloomy air; there was silence, then it *plooked* down.

"What was that?" a voice said.

I froze, then shrank back into the bushes.

"What was what?" a second voice answered. One of them coughed.

"Like a splash or something." The voices of two men came from up by the freeway bridge. Maybe even underneath it.

"Freakin' fish. This is a river." More coughing.

There was silence. I could hear their boots on rocks. Something glass shattered against the concrete. A stick scraped stone. "Looks like maybe they stopped here, but they musta kept going."

"Too bad," said the other man.

"They had money on them, I just know it."

"Money, schmoney. I liked that young chick." Cough.

"With the weird hair and all those earrings? Are you kidding?"

"They say those kind are wilder."

The two laughed. One of them coughed again.

"How old do you think she was?" said the first voice.

"Old enough."

Both men guffawed. More deep coughing.

There was a pause. "Gimme one of those."

Another pause, a brief popping sound, then the smell of cigarette smoke.

"Hey, better luck next time," one of them said, and the sound of their boots and coughing receded up the bank. From the freeway came the rattle of a tractor engine; then it, too, receded. I peeked out from the bushes. The dark cab of the tractor shrank out of sight beyond the freeway embankment.

So much for friendly country folks. I let out a long breath. I sat for a while until the shaky feeling went away. Then I made my way back to the campsite. My parents' tent was quiet. When I slipped inside ours, Sarah was breathing steadily and evenly. In the darkness I could see the pale shape of her favorite stuffed animal, a battered white rabbit named Knuckles, tucked against her black T-shirt. I lay there in my sleeping bag with my eyes open for a long time. I kept imagining I could smell cigarette smoke.

In the morning I woke up with a start. Sarah lay there with her mouth open making little snoring sounds. The sides of the tent breathed back and forth, too, in the breeze. Silence.

I poked out my head to check the wind. River fog had scrubbed the air, leaving it dust free and fresh; I sucked in a deep breath. A small hawk, perched on the irrigator pipe, flapped away at my movement—and a striped gopher, equally startled, sat up on its haunches, then dove into its hole.

"Sorry, guy," I murmured to the hawk. I got up and looked around, checked for tracks. A deer had passed down the trail in the night. In the dust its small hoofprints were like little hearts strung on an invisible thread. I eased down the river. Across, on the far bank, an eagle was perched in a dead tree. I saw it only by its sudden motion—a flash of white and brown—as it flapped away. It had seen me first. *If you want to learn the woods, learn to wait. Find yourself a log or a stump and sit there all day, sunrise to sunset. Be quiet and watch. The whole forest will come past your spot. One day, without moving, is all it takes. But it will be the hardest thing you've ever done.* I peered through the bushes toward the freeway bridge, but it was still and empty.

When I returned, my parents were up and around at their tent site. Nat already had the camp stove fired up.

"Did you hear anything last night?" I asked casually.

"What time?" Nat replied.

"Not long after you went to bed."

"Maybe," she said, squinting to remember. "It was like an engine sound? Yes. I think so."

I was silent.

"Why? What was it?"

"Nothing. No problem," I said.

My mother looked about. "Well, it looks like good weather," she said. "The sooner we get on the road, the sooner we can get to Birch Bay."

"Suits me," my father said, and yawned loudly. "The breeze is decent. I can work with it."

I glanced toward the freeway. "I'm not sure about traveling in daylight."

"Hey, we're out of the big bad city," my father replied. There was a trace of sarcasm in his voice.

"Yeah, well," I said, then let it slide. I didn't want to scare them. And besides, the day did look great: The sun was going to shine, and the wind was already picking up from the west.

"It feels like we're so close," my mother said. "Tonight we could sleep in the cabin."

"Light a fire in the old fireplace, take a dip in the lake," my father said.

They looked at me. What could I say? I shrugged.

"Okay. I guess."

"Go wake up Sarah," my mother said happily.

I walked back to the tent and with pleasure gave Sarah's sleeping bag a yank. She woke up with funny hair and crabby; I laughed at her. Someday I might tell her how I saved her from the bad guys. But she probably wouldn't believe me.

By eight A.M. we were on the road to the Brainerd lakes area. Another forty or so highway miles, a few winding dirt roads, and then Birch Bay. My job, as always, would be to enter the cabin first. I had to chase out whatever varmints—usually a mouse, once a pair of gray squirrels, another time a little owl—had taken up residence. *A place goes empty—a den, a nest, a hole in the ground—and other critters move in. That's how nature works.*

Shooing them out of the cabin was an easy job, plus I got a lot of mileage from it. The rest of my family was scared of anything small that crawled, chewed, buzzed, or flapped its wings. After we arrived and I did my varmint duty, I planned to relax and be worthless—like a sixteen-year-old is supposed to be.

The breeze held fairly steady. Even Sarah took a turn on the boom sail. The sun brightened from orange to white-yellow as it rose higher, and the road was clear and open. My mother switched on her Palm Pal to radio. I was hoping for some music, but no such luck:

> . . . *indicators point to a second summer of record-low crop yields in the United States corn belt and the wheat-growing regions of Russia. This is coupled with the fact that world food supplies—mainly wheat and corn—throughout history have never held more than two years' stock in reserve. The result? Widespread hoarding of essential food supplies, including water.*

"This is news?" I muttered. Even as the analyst droned on, the *Ali Princess* drew even with a long field where a farmer's tractor kicked up a swirl of dust. He was cultivating row crops of some kind—probably potatoes, but it was hard to tell. The plants were runty and limp.

. . . clearly an overreaction, brought on, some would say, by the news media. After all, world staples such as bananas and soybeans still grow fine in warmer regions, particularly near the equator.

"I haven't seen a banana, let alone California lettuce, for over a year," my mother said.

We all looked at the farmer's field. At the dusty, shrimpy plants.

. . . problem is not necessarily food supplies but distribution. As transportation costs soar, how do we get strawberries to Cincinnati, oranges to Minneapolis, apples to Winnipeg?

"Will you turn that thing off?" I said suddenly.

My mother blinked and turned.

"We don't need to hear that stuff!" I said. I tried to stick with the facts. Food stores were still fairly well stocked, though mainly with canned stuff, which was not a good sign. I also was pretty sure that a third year without a good crop, and Dara Jamison might be right: Pets, watch out. "All the news does is make people depressed. Who needs that?"

"Easy, brother Miles," Sarah teased. She knew that I hated the news. Those endlessly talking heads, their droning voices using too many words.

"Okay, you have a point there," my mother said. "How about some music?" She tuned to another radio station—classic rock, of course.

"Do we have to listen to *that*?" Sarah said instantly.

"Easy, sister Sarah."

"How about some jazz?" my father said softly. "Try down around ninety-five."

My mother rolled the dial. "—was the Shawnee Kingston Jazz Band," the announcer finished, "from their tribute to the Buddy Rich CD. Next up, a classic set from John Coltrane."

We all looked at my father.

He was silent a moment. "Maybe Miles is right," he said. There was something incredibly sad in his voice. My mother clicked off the sound altogether.

"Anyway, Birch Bay tonight, gang," she said, stowing her Palm Pal and trying to pick up the mood.

No one said anything.

See what the news does? I wanted to say.

For the next half hour we rolled along at a good pace,

and even I, the family pessimist, started to relax a bit. We might actually get there alive. Once we got to the cabin, we'd unload our food, including several big bags of rice. The lake was full of fish, and I knew how to catch them. There was firewood, there was fresh water. We'd be fine.

Heading north, with a quartering westerly breeze in the sail, we approached the entrance to Camp Ripley, a longtime center of National Guard activity. As a kid I used to think the convoys of trucks were cool because they were painted in camo. But lately trucks like that made me uneasy.

An armed sentry at the head of the long camp driveway stepped out onto the highway and held up his arm. We had no choice but to dump the sail and coast to a stop. My mother hopped off the *Ali Princess* well before we reached a complete halt.

"Hello there," the soldier said to her.

"Why are you stopping us?" she said. She was suddenly in the face of the young soldier. "This is a public highway, right?"

"I'm not really—" he began.

"Is there some particular law we're breaking?" she asked.

"Well, my orders are to check on folks—"

"Correct me if I'm wrong, but I don't recall the United States Constitution being amended lately, particularly Article Twelve, which guarantees citizens the right of free passage. You do know the Constitution, don't you?"

A small convoy of trucks approached and signaled a turn onto the highway—which we blocked.

"Um, have a nice trip, ma'am," the soldier stammered, and stepped aside.

"That's more like it," my mother said, shaking her finger at him. "Just because this country's struggling a bit doesn't mean you guys are in charge, remember that!"

"No ma'am, I mean, yes ma'am," he called out, and waved the trucks forward.

We pedaled a few yards until we caught the wind.

"I don't remember an Article Twelve," I ventured. I had studied the Constitution in civics class; Article Twelve did not ring a bell.

"Me neither," Sarah said.

"Well, if there's not an Article Twelve, there ought to be one," my mother said.

By noon the wind had dropped, as had our speed. It was getting warm, too, another reason I had not wanted to move during the day. All four of us pedaled steadily. Sarah kept drinking water as if our supply was endless.

"Take a break soon?" my father asked. Little rivulets of sweat and dust leaked out the sides of his mask.

"Rock Lake is just ahead," I called. It was a small town where we always stopped for ice cream.

"Maybe the Dairy Queen is open," Sarah panted.

"Yeah, well, if it is, let's check the prices first," my mother said.

Soon, just off the expressway, behind a grove of dusty pines, rose the red-and-white water tower of Rock Lake. Its round top was painted like a fishing bobber.

"I see it," Sarah said. "I saw it first."

Not true, but I didn't say anything.

We turned off the expressway and pedaled toward Main Street—which was blocked. A wooden barricade sat across the entrance to town, manned by an old fellow slumped in a lawn chair and wearing sunglasses. LOCAL TRAFFIC ONLY read the sign on the barricade. Beyond, down Main Street, a few people came and went on riding lawnmowers and small garden tractors.

We pulled to a stop. The old man jerked upright in his chair; he had been dozing. He stared at the *Princess* as if he was dreaming. "Whoa! What do we have here?"

Several locals stepped from the nearby bakery to look at the *Princess*. Three teenagers, each driving a muddy four-wheeler, roared up. Wearing full helmets and dark goggles, the drivers peered at the *Princess* and raced their engines.

My mother ignored the local Hell's Angels kids. "Good afternoon," she said to the gatekeeper. "Is the Dairy Queen open?"

"Yes. Why?" the old-timer said.

"We thought we'd stop for some ice cream," my mother said.

The old man's gaze went to our luggage in the cargo bay. "You're not from here?"

"Yes and no," she said. "We have a cabin just up the road a ways. That's where we're headed."

"A cabin? Where?"

"It's on County Road 77, north side of Gull Lake."

"Where on the north side of Gull Lake?" one of the teenagers called; he gunned the engine of his lawn tractor.

"Just a half mile past the golf course."

The men looked at each other. One of them shrugged.

"Okay, then," the old man said. He pulled aside the barrier with a scraping sound. "Otherwise I'd have to ask you to get on that crazy rig and head back where you came from. We already got too many people coming up here from the cities."

"Too many," another rough-looking guy echoed.

"Have a nice day," Sarah said as we passed by. The four-wheeler posse made two loud loops around us and raced their engines while we parked.

"Losers," Sarah muttered.

The Dairy Queen clerk was a middle-aged woman wearing a little red-and-white hat. There was only vanilla ice cream, and no cones, but sundaes were possible.

"And how much might these sundaes be?" my mother asked.

"Ah, four sundaes? That would be $32.00." The clerk looked at my mother without smiling.

"I always said this town was a tourist trap," my mother murmured to my father. Then she looked up. "All right. Four sundaes. And don't spare the ice cream."

In the end they weren't that big. As we ate, some locals watched us.

"Strangers," Sarah said to them. "That's us."

They stared blankly.

I kicked her sharply under the table. "Don't," I said. I didn't like being here. Outside, the four-wheelers kept making circles around the *Princess*. I felt like that carp with its fin out of the water.

"Eat up," I said to my family.

As we left Rock Lake, the whining four-wheeler brigade was nowhere to been seen. That was fine by me. We picked up the pace on the *Ali Princess* and quickly put Rock Lake a couple of miles behind. Maybe it was the energy boost from the ice cream, or maybe it was because we were almost to Birch Bay, but we finally found our pedaling rhythm. Another hour at the most. I began to daydream about a nap on the wide lakefront porch. . . .

"Miles!" my father shouted.

"Oh, God!" Sarah chirped.

In a whine of engines and a blue cloud of oil smoke, a half dozen four-wheelers broke out of the trees and raced alongside us. Two of them, ones I hadn't seen in Rock Lake, were driven by larger guys; plastic rifle scabbards jutted from the rear.

"Keep going!" I shouted to my family.

The gang matched our pace, then sped ahead. I thought they were leaving—until they turned sharply, skidded to a stop, and blocked the highway. We had nowhere to go.

And the *Ali Princess* had no real brakes.

"Drag your feet!" I cried. We did, and managed to stop just inches short of a muddy, battered vehicle with balloon tires.

"What is this?" my mother said. As usual, she hopped off the *Ali Princess* and stepped forward.

"This is a toll road," the biggest driver said. He glanced to the others, who nodded. We could see none of their faces. I looked again at the rifle scabbards.

"No, it's a public highway," my mother said.

"Not today it isn't," another rider said.

"Go easy," my father murmured to her. He, too, was looking at the gun cases. He stepped forward.

"Hey, young dudes," he said easily. I recognized his stage voice, his musician's manner. "What's going on? We're headed up to our place on the lake."

"Fine. Pay us and you can be on your way."

My father smiled. "You guys need a few bucks for ice cream, maybe a little gasoline, I can understand that. Hey, all you got to do is ask."

I understood—maybe for the first time since I was small and saw him sail the *Tonka Miss* all day against the wind—that my father knew how to do a lot of things. It was just that he was totally different from me.

"So, we're asking," the leader said him.

"Okay," my father replied. He kept his voice light and amused. He wagged a finger as he counted the riders. "Six of you. How about five bucks apiece. Thirty bucks." Without waiting for an answer, he reached into his shirt pocket and peeled off three tens. He held out the money. The leader snatched it.

"Now we got some miles to cover, and you boys have a nice day," my father said. He jerked his head for us to get ready to pedal.

The lead bandit looked at the money in his hand. "Seems to me if you got thirty, then you must have a hundred."

There was silence.

"Or three hundred," another said. They all laughed.

"In fact, why don't we take all your money?" the leader said.

I looked at my baseball bat. One against six was not good.

"Listen, boys," my father began.

"You listen to me. I want you all to step off that crazy vehicle," the leader said. The others nodded.

"So much for traveling in broad daylight," I muttered.

The hijackers dismounted and pulled narrow wooden

clubs from their rifle scabbards. At least there weren't real guns.

"Step aside," the leader said.

We obeyed.

Just as the gang was about to ransack the *Princess*—like in an old cowboy movie—the sheriff arrived. Not really the sheriff, but a single green Humvee with its headlights on.

"Shit!" the leader said. The gang whirled around to look at the Humvee. In one motion they leaped onto their little iron horses and cranked the engines. Within seconds they lurched forward and roared up the bank and into the trees. Their dust hung in the air.

The Humvee approached, then braked to a stop. "Hello, folks." The driver wore mirrored sunglasses.

My father nodded.

"Was that that gang of little shits on four-wheelers?" the Humvee driver said, looking at the dust cloud and the tracks up the bank.

"I would say that was them," my father said.

"Their ass is grass," the Humvee passenger said. "We've had nothing but trouble with that bunch."

"They did seem a little short on structured summer activities," my mother said. My heart was still pounding.

"Tell you what," the Humvee driver said. "We'll give you folks an escort for a few miles just to make sure you're safe. In fact, I've got a tow rope. Why don't you hook on?"

"Miles?" my mother said.

The government never did anything for me, that's for sure. Most people depend on the government. Not me. I depended on myself.

"Sure," I said.

"Thank you," my mother said to the soldier. As we hooked on and got ready for our free ride, she glanced at me and shrugged. "Crow is not that bad to eat. As an adult, you get used to it."

"Excuse me?" the Humvee driver said to her.

"An inside joke," my mother said.

"Ready!" I called to the driver. And with a small lurch we were off. We kicked back and let the breeze blow over us as we rolled north.

BUENA VISTA REVISITED

THE ORAL-HISTORY PROJECT CONTINUED FOR six weeks. Six times I visited Mr. Kurz. Mainly we worked on things. Sometimes he talked, sometimes he didn't. Unlike most of the other ninth graders, I didn't bother with a tape recorder. I didn't even take notes. I could remember what I needed to. And anyway, most of it was rambling, useless stuff.

Berries. A man should know his berries. Best ones are blueberries. If they can escape a late frost in June, you're lucky. But they're hardy plants. They don't need a lot of sunlight, plus they grow best where there are pine trees and the soil is sandy. Blueberries like pine needles for some reason. Makes the soil sour, is my theory. You want to find blueberries, look for pines, rocks, and sand. But they don't last long. If the bears don't get them, by the end of July, they're done.

Wild grapes last a little longer. Look for them along riverbanks and swamps. The vines use other trees to climb up and get better light. They depend on other trees. Kind of like most people depend on the government. Parasites, I call them. But wild grapes are mighty tasty. Most times you got to look high up and climb for them, but they're worth it.

High-bush cranberries last the longest—again, if the birds or bears don't get them. They come in red clusters. You'll see them in September, where it's swampy, hanging from bushes a tall man high. Sometimes you can smell cranberries before you see them—kind of a rank, sweet odor. They're good all fall and into the winter, even if they freeze. Once when I was trapping in January, I saw some bushes red with them. Those berries were as hard and clear as agates. I picked them, but I had nothing to carry them in except my hat, which I had to put back on my head 'cause it was cold. When I got home, the heat of my skull had thawed the berries and red juice was running *down my neck. I looked like I'd been in a fight with a bear. I made jelly that night. Whole cabin smelled of it, hot and tangy.*

Okay, fine. I could do something with the bear part. Maybe make up that the bear had broken into his cabin. Hand-to-hand combat. Who was going to know? Plus I'd heard that Litzke graded mainly on volume. Some kids said he had a scale and weighed the final project: The heavier the interview, the more the pages, the better the grade.

My brothers, my whole family, they always thought I was crazy. Just because I lived alone and saved my money. Not like them, with credit cards and house payments and fancy cars. I told them, when you pay interest, you're working for the bank. Banks are like prisons—you just can't see the walls. They said I was nuts. Just because I never had a credit card in my life, and no house payment, either. Nuts, they called me. But that's how I could live so cheap—I never paid any interest to nobody. But you live like a hermit, they told me. Maybe so, but I'll bet I got more money put away than you do, I told them. Which was a mistake. You never want to tell anybody—not even your own family—what you got. Because once you tell, you're a marked man.

Mr. Litzke took great pleasure in asking me how Mr. Kurz and I were getting along.

"Fine," I told him.

Once he dropped by Mr. Kurz's room to check on us. Luckily I managed to hide my tools.

"Well, are you two getting a lot of work done?" he asked loudly.

"A lot," I said. So far Mr. Kurz and I had repaired four skateboards, and I had cleared a total of eighty bucks reselling them.

Mr. Kurz stared suspiciously at Litzke. We were all silent.

"Carry on, then," Litzke said.

After he left, Mr. Kurz muttered, "Who was that guy?"

"He works for the government," I whispered.

"That's what I thought," Mr. Kurz said.

They never found me, though. They came up north and were snooping around, asking, but no one knew where my cabin was. That's because it wasn't on the tax roll. He, he, he. Why buy your own land when there's thousands of acres of it just sitting there? State lands belong to the people. And that's me, I'm the people. A veteran, too. In the War I fought in Italy, Germany, France, you name it. Before the War I was different. I liked people. But when it was over in forty-five, all I wanted was a little peace and quiet. So I went up north and found me a spot on the river and built me a shack on the Mississippi. Near Itasca Park, that's all I'll say. Better than a shack. A nice little cabin. No roads to it, either—but you could get to it by car. He, he, he. That's all I'll say about that. Anyway, when my family couldn't find me, they had to leave me alone. Which is the way I wanted it. I lived by myself for over fifty years. Happy as a clam, too. My mistake was coming down to the city for my sister's funeral. She got old and died. Don't know how that happened. But she was the only nice one among my brothers and sisters, so I took the Greyhound bus down from Bemidji. I was eighty-nine myself by then. They were waiting for me, oh yes. All smiles. I should have known something was up. After the funeral they said, Hans, we want you to stay on with us. No thanks, I said. They said, You can't go on anymore living like you do, like a wild man, like a hermit—look at you, they said. I said I liked my life just fine. They said, We have a place for you here in the city. A place of your own, they said. They kept smiling. All smiles. That night I slipped out of the house, tried to walk to the Greyhound bus station. But I got turned around. Every street looked the same. I couldn't remember which direction anything was. I didn't know which way was home. I just wanted to get back up north to my cabin. But the police found me, took me back to my brother's place. And here I am. At Buena Vista. What kind of name is Buena Vista, anyway? That's what I want to know.

"It's Spanish," I said as I tightened a truck nut. "It means beautiful view." I kept working. I hadn't been listening closely.

Then I felt him staring at me, and I looked up. His beady blue eyes had swelled with water. His heavy lower lids were like two dams ready to break and let their rivers flow. Suddenly he turned away from me. He went to his armchair and sat staring out the window.

SQUATTERS

AFTER A FIVE-MILE TOW FROM the friendly soldiers, we unhooked at County Road 77. "We'll take it from here," I said.

The soldiers saluted and went on their way.

"Well, that worked out well," Nat said.

We laughed at her, then pointed the *Princess* down the familiar curving dirt road. After our rest, we pedaled quickly uphill and down, like runners in their final kick. Panting, we rolled up the last hill, the trees close along both sides of the road, then arrived at our driveway. We were all laughing and smiling. Sarah hopped off and ran to the mailbox. "Who knows, maybe I have mail already!"

"Knowing your friends, I wouldn't doubt it," I said. Sarah's group gave new meaning to the word codependency.

The mailbox door squeaked open. Sarah's hand emerged with some envelopes. She stared at them. "There is mail."

My mother frowned and stepped forward.

"They're addressed to somebody named Kleinke," Sarah said. "And here's one for a D. Tolber."

"Must be a mistake," my mother said. She took the envelopes from Sarah and looked at them.

My eyes went to the driveway. There was a recent tire track, possibly a motorcycle, in the powdery dirt. I squinted up the narrow, curving driveway.

"Or there might be somebody here," I murmured.

"Where?" my mother said.

I nodded toward the driveway, and pointed to the tire tracks in the ash.

"Well, there better not be," my mother said, and began to walk quickly up the driveway. We hurried to catch up.

Soon, through the trees, we saw the brown roofline.

Then the glint of window glass and the coppery log front of the cabin. But in the yard everything was changed. We drew up to stare.

A car, a late-model sedan, was parked on the side and covered with ash. Another older car, without wheels, sat halfway into the trees. A large, shiny Harley perched on the porch; its wheel tracks in the ashy driveway led right up the wooden steps, which looked chewed and splintered.

To the left, hanging on the clothesline (we never had a clothesline), was somebody's wash. Lots of kids' clothes. Behind the house came the *chak* sound of an axe splitting wood. Some kind of animal went "*baa!*" There were laughing voices of little kids. Only the lake was the same. Gull Lake sparkled—as always—in the sunlight.

"What the hell is going on here!" my mother yelled. She stalked forward.

"Wait. Nat! Go carefully!" my father said.

But that only made my mother pick up her pace. We followed her. After all, it was our cabin.

She thumped onto the porch, grabbed the screen door, and strode inside. The house smelled of cooking, garlic in particular. By the fireplace a couple of small children were playing cars and dolls on the stone floor;

when Nat burst in, they screamed and ran for the back door.

They were normal-looking little kids in summer clothes; the girl, a redhead about four years old, turned, rushed back, grabbed a monkey doll, and rushed away again. We heard them calling, "Momma! Daddy! Danny!"

Soon a man rushed inside; he was shirtless, pale and out of shape.

"What are *you* doing in our house?" Sarah said. She had stepped ahead of my mother.

The man swallowed and looked behind him. A woman holding a baby appeared. She looked like an ordinary mother.

"Your house?" the woman said. Something caught in her voice.

"That's right," my mother said. "I'm Natalie Newell, this is my family, and you're in our cabin."

"Listen," the man began, stammering slightly. "I'm Rick and this is my wife, Ruth. Kleinke is our last name."

"We could care less who you are," Sarah said, her voice getting hysterical. "Get out!"

My father quickly put his arm around Sarah. "Easy, easy now," he murmured. He looked at Rick and Ruth.

"We can work this out, I'm sure," he said with his stage voice. He even managed a smile.

The man's wife, Ruth, did not smile. She looked stunned. "I always knew this would happen."

Her words stiffened the man's posture. "We've been here for nearly a year," he said, as if that was supposed to explain everything.

"And now it's time for you and your family to leave," my mother said.

The man named Rick frowned. "Things are different now."

"Yes, that's right, different," his wife murmured. Her eyes flickered to the floor, then back up.

"Hey—what the hell's going on here?" a louder voice boomed. A large man came in from the deck. He wore a black T-shirt that covered his big chest but not his round belly; a red bandana held back long stringy hair. His full beard was peppered with sawdust, and he held an axe.

"The owners. They've arrived," Rick said.

"Well, well, well," the burly man said. He set down his axe. Alongside him appeared another woman who was dressed like him—they looked like a biker couple. She also had wood chips on her black, sleeveless T-shirt. She had no bra on, that was clear.

"So the absentee owners finally appear," the man said with a grin.

"The phone?" my mother said. "I need to make a call."

"You should know where it is," the man said. He narrowed his eyes.

Nat went to the knotty-pine wall cabinet and opened it up.

"Right here," she said, turning to show everyone. She picked up the receiver, punched in three numbers. I guessed they were 911. Then she held the receiver to her ear.

The bigger man chuckled.

"It's dead," Nat said, turning to him.

"You asked if there was a phone," he said, "not if it works."

"Danny, don't," the biker's wife said softly. She had a surprisingly nice voice.

There was silence again. All of us looked at each other; nobody spoke. By now the children, including two more for a total of five, peeked out from behind the adults.

"I'm sorry, but if you don't agree to leave, we'll have to get the sheriff," my mother said. She looked to my father, whose brown eyes blinked rapidly, as if he was cranking through all possible solutions.

The woman holding the baby spoke up. "The sheriff is my brother," she said. She said it softly and evenly.

My mother stared.

"He said it was all right for us to stay here. We're from Chicago, and we couldn't stay there, not in the city, not with the children, so we came here," she continued in a rush. "You don't know how bad things were—"

"That's enough," her husband said. He glanced toward his children.

"Things is different nowadays," Danny added. "The rules have changed."

"And who are you?" my mother asked, turning to the biker. Her city voice was returning, which worried me.

"Me and Sheila, we're the real squatters," big Danny said. He had teeth missing on top. "We were here first, and then Rick and Ruth came along with their three kids and we took them in."

"You took them in," my mother said, her voice rising.

"That's right," the big man said easily. "A nice big place like this, just sitting empty—hell, there was room for two families."

My mother narrowed her eyes in her I'm-counting-to-ten mode.

"I'll tell you what," she said to the people in our cabin. "I don't care if the sheriff is your uncle, your brother, or the Pope. I suggest you start packing."

"Easy, Nat," my father said.

"Daddy, do we have to leave again?" one of the children whimpered.

"Shhh!" Ruth said.

The "guests" looked at each other. The big man's gaze flickered to the children. The place was absolutely silent except a couple of sharp *baa-baa*'s out back.

"Tell you what," my father said. He smiled. "We're going to head outside and bring our vehicle up into the yard, start unpacking ourselves a bit. There's no rush here—as long as we all understand what needs to be done."

The biker wife, Sheila, cocked her head oddly as my father spoke. "Newell, Newell," she said. "Hey—you're not Artie Newell of the Shawnee Kingston band?"

My father did a quick hambone slap on his leg. "That's me."

"I'll be damned," Sheila said. She turned to Danny. "You know the Shawnee Kingston Jazz Band."

"Yeah. So?" Danny said.

There was silence.

"See you in a bit, then," my father said. He looked at us and jerked his head toward the door.

We walked down the steps—our wooden steps—and back up the driveway. It was like we were zombies. Sarah blurted, "They just can't take our cabin. People can't do that!"

"Of course not, dear," my mother said. "Actually, they'll probably be gone by tonight."

My father and I exchanged glances.

I lowered the mast on the *Princess*, which took a few minutes, and then we pedaled her down the long, winding driveway. When we rolled into the yard, all the children's faces popped up at the windows. They gaped at the *Princess* like she was a giant toy.

"Let's give them some time," my father said, purposefully not looking at the cabin.

We slowly unloaded much of the *Princess*, making sure to talk normally. To act as if we belonged here.

But there was no movement from the cabin. No luggage appeared on the porch. After almost a half hour my father shrugged. "Well, plan B," he said. He headed toward the cabin.

We followed.

At the screen door my father paused to knock.

"Why are we knocking on our own—" my mother began.

"Please," my father said. "Let's try this my way, all right?"

My mother stared at him but was silent.

We stepped inside. The squatters were all sitting at the table—our table—ready to eat supper. A large kettle of soup steamed off a meaty smell, and there was a big basket of what looked to be homemade bread. And a jar of pickles. And a big glass jug of milk. They all looked up at us from the table.

"Well then," my father began.

No one said anything. For once I was really glad not to be an adult.

The biker's wife, Sheila, looked at Sarah and me; I had been staring at the food.

"You children hungry?" she asked.

I swallowed.

"No, they're most certainly not," my mother said. "We have food of our own."

My father gave her a glare like I'd never seen. Then he nodded at Sheila. "Maybe that's what we need. Sit down at the table and talk this out."

It was the weirdest dinner I've ever been at. Sarah

ended up sitting by Danny. She kept edging away from him. But there was plenty of great food, including venison stew. Even Sarah, who loves animals, ate some of it. The bread, thick and wheaty and still warm, was fabulous. My mother refused to touch a bite. I felt terrible eating in front of her, but I couldn't stop. Nobody said anything. We just ate. I had honey on my bread, and a glass of milk to wash everything down. At the first taste of the milk, however, I wanted to spew. It was thick and creamy—like no milk I'd ever tasted.

"Goat's milk." Big Danny chuckled hoarsely. "It'll put hair on your chest, kid."

My throat clenched and closed up, but I forced myself to down the rest like I'd been drinking goat's milk all my life. Gaah!

Slowly people stopped sneaking looks at each other and started to talk.

"People were killed right next door to us in Chicago," Ruth said. "We heard the screams. The gunshots."

"And we lived in a good suburb," her husband added.

"So I finally got in touch with my brother, the sheriff, and he said come here, but make it soon. Somehow he'd try to find a place for us."

"Our place," my mother remarked.

My father nudged her with his elbow.

"There are vacant homes and cabins like this one all around the lakes here," Ruth said to her.

"Were," said Danny. "They're all full now."

"It's funny how many people in the Midwest have two homes," Rick continued, "one in the city and then a lake cabin."

"Daddy, how can you live in two homes at the same time?" one of the kids asked.

There was silence again.

"We're not criminals," Ruth said. There was a kind of pleading in her voice. "We're just trying to survive. Like everybody else. And here was this nice, empty cabin—"

"I wouldn't say 'empty,'" Danny said. A laugh rumbled in his big belly.

Ruth colored slightly. "They—Danny and Sheila and their two kids—were already living here."

"Let's say visiting here," my mother qualified.

"The sheriff said that if we took them in," Sheila said, "he wouldn't charge us with breaking and entering. It was a deal that worked for everybody. And as Danny said, all of us get along, the kids especially, so we're just working together and trying to get through these times."

"Well, I'm afraid you're going to have to get through

these times somewhere else," my mother said.

"Do we have to leave?" the four-year-old girl pleaded.

Both my mother and Danny began to speak, but Ruth quickly interrupted them both. "Your family must have a home?" she said to us.

"We do, in Minneapolis," my father said. "But it's the same story—people are getting a little crazy. It feels dangerous."

"Anybody killed in your neighborhood?" Rick asked.

"Well, no, but—"

"Then it's not like where we came from," Ruth said firmly.

There was silence.

"Do we have to leave?" the little girl whined again.

"No," Danny growled, "none of *us* are leaving."

We camped that evening in our own yard. Ruth and Sheila were helpful, making sure we had water from the pump—an outdoor hand pump, which was new—and that the goats were tied so they wouldn't bother us. I kept trying to hate these people. I certainly hated Danny the biker. But Ruth and Sheila—hating them was more difficult. Even the five kids weren't that bad. They kept creeping closer to the *Princess*, so finally I let them climb on her. They took the seats and bounced up and down and pretended they were pedaling and made wild kid noises. Even the goats were kind of nice. They had nice brown eyes and weird droopy ears, and they wanted to nibble everything. One named Emily kept nuzzling and bumping Sarah, and leaning into her fingers when she scratched behind her ears. From the porch Sheila said, "Emily likes you." My sister blinked and looked up suddenly—at our cabin, at all the strangers—as if she had forgotten where she was. Then she burst into tears and disappeared into our tent. The little kids looked around as if they'd done something wrong.

Later, in the tent, Sarah read a vampire novel by candlelight. She held the book very close to her face. I lay there and listened to night sounds. The waves lapping on the beach. The nuzzling, bumping sounds of the goats. A *whoo-whoo* of a faraway owl. Sarah's pages rustling as they turned. And, from the other tent, my parents' voices. As they got louder, I sat up in my bag to hear them better. Sarah looked up too.

"So what do you suggest we do?" my father said. "Get a gun and shoot them all?"

"I wish," Sarah muttered.

There was silence; then I heard the muffled sounds

of my mother crying. Sarah and I stared at each other. I
don't know that we'd ever heard our mother cry.

"I'm sorry," my father mumbled.

"It's okay," she said, her voice unsteady. "It's just that
I feel so bad for their children. But we've got our own to
worry about—"

"Shhhh," my father said gently. "Shhhh . . ."

After a while my mother's Palm Pal came on. The
tiny crackle of news reports fell just below good hearing,
which was all right by me. Once my mother said,
"Greenbriar Lane. My God. We may have left just in
time."

Sarah and I looked at each other.

"Do you know what, Miles?"

"What?"

"That creep Danny? Under the table he put his hand
on my leg."

I was silent. "I'm sorry," I said finally. I felt stupid.
Like I should do something nice for her. Sarah blew
out the candle and zipped herself into her bag. After a
while she rolled closer, so our backs touched just a little.
I moved too, so they were firm against each other. It felt
good that way, like when we were kids. And warmer,
too.

In the dark she whispered, "What are we gonna do now, Miles? If they don't leave, what's going to happen to us?"

"Hey, they'll leave. And if they don't, we'll figure something out," I said. I used my father's everything-will-be-cool voice.

"Promise?"

"Poke a stick up my nose, where it stops, nobody knows." It was a stupid saying from when we were kids.

Sarah managed a tiny laugh, then fell asleep almost instantly. I, too, begin to relax. I was just drifting off—the lake sounds were like a lullaby—when I smelled cigarette smoke. I sat up with a jerk. A soft, steady squeaking sound came from the porch. I peeked out of the tent flap. Danny sat in the shadows on the porch, rocking and smoking. The red eye of his cigarette grew and shrank.

Grew and shrank.

It was like this was war and he had the night watch.

MEMORY BOOK

BACK IN NINTH GRADE, AFTER the oral-history interviews were finished, I didn't go back to see Mr. Kurz. My memory book, however, was a masterpiece. I constructed fantastic stories of Mr. Kurz as a war hero, a ruthless Nazi-killing machine. After World War II he became a big-game hunter and traveled the world. Along the way he made friends with such people as Ernest Hemingway and John Wayne. Later in life he became a conservationist, giving away all his money to groups focused on saving the animals and protecting the environment. He was a kindly, happy man who loved his government, dogs, and children.

A couple of days after I turned in the memory book, Litzke had me stay after class. "What is this?" he said, holding up the memory book.

"It's the oral-history assignment."

"Whose oral history?" he said. He fanned through the pages as if they had a bad smell.

"Mr. Kurz," I said. "He's the one you assigned me to, right?"

Mr. Litzke looked up at me. "What if I went and had a little talk with Mr. Kurz?" he said. One eyebrow arched in a look that said, *Your ass is grass, Newell.*

"If you have any doubts, then I think you should talk to him," I said. I kept my eyes round and innocent looking.

"I will," Litzke said. "After school. Today."

The next day when I came to class, Litzke said nothing to me. In fact, he purposely would not look at me.

I couldn't resist. I raised my hand. "Mr. Litzke? Did you have a chance to speak with Mr. Kurz?"

Litzke turned, gave me the world's blackest look, then continued with our lesson. It was a major victory for me. Nathan Schmidt gave me a high five. We had great fun imagining Litzke—who, as a teacher, technically did work for the government—showing up at Buena Vista in his short-sleeved white shirt and skinny black tie, and quizzing Mr. Kurz about his life.

However, sometimes a major victory is not all it's cracked up to be. I felt bad about fictionalizing the memory book. Not bad as in guilt-ridden and sleepless, but bad in a low-grade, continuing way, like—kind of like a grain of sand in my sock. It was one of the reasons why I didn't walk into Buena Vista to see Mr. Kurz. But there were other reasons. My friends, the ash fall, my father being gone all the time—something always got in the way. Then when the economy went belly-up and life in the suburbs turned scary, I spent all my spare time building the *Ali Princess*.

It was during those late nights in the garage that I began to think again about Mr. Kurz. As I worked, sometimes I heard his voice inside my head.

Maybe try a socket instead of that wrench.

Are you sure you want to cut that off so short?

Take your time. Rush and you'll only skin your knuckles.

We need a new bolt. This one ain't worth a tinker's damn.

Sometimes his voice was so loud I would suddenly look up; it was as if he had been right beside me, or at least somewhere in the shadows of the shop. On one of those nights I promised myself that, when the *Ali Princess* was done, I would go back to see Mr. Kurz.

Buena Vista looked just the same, only smaller. And dustier. Nobody sat outside in wheelchairs. I guessed the dust was too much.

I thought of checking in at the main desk but decided against it. I would slip in and out, no commotion, no tracks. Mr. Kurz would approve. I eased around the corner and headed down the hall. The place had the same sickly clean smell, the same old-timers slumped in wheelchairs, the same moans and groans as I had remembered. I thought I'd take a chance and see if Mr. Kurz was in his same room. As I approached it, I took a deep breath. His door was open.

I paused, then stepped forward. Inside was a jumble of chairs and a pile of mattresses. I stared. Mr. Kurz's room was now a storeroom. I felt like somebody had punched me in the gut. I backed away, into the hallway.

"Hey, don't I know you?" said a passing voice.

I spun around. It was the male nurse. His hair was much longer now but he still wore the same white outfit and white tennis shoes. He stopped and smiled.

"Miles," I said. "Miles Newell. I did my ninth-grade

oral-history project with Mr. Kurz."

"Sure, I remember," he said. We shook hands. Then he glanced to the storeroom, and back to me. His smile slipped. "Bad news, Miles."

I took a small breath and held it.

"Mr. Kurz died about a month ago."

"Shit," I said. The word just popped out—the same one that most airplane pilots say just before they crash—the same one that shows up again and again on cockpit voice recorders recovered from crash sites. Usually it's their last word. Shit.

"Yes, I hear you," the nurse said. "As old-timers go, I didn't mind Mr. Kurz one bit."

I stood there taking in little breaths and letting them out.

"His family was worthless, though," the nurse continued. "We called them several times, but in the end we had to do all the arrangements ourselves."

"Arrangements?"

"Get him to the funeral home. Make sure he was cremated—that's what he wanted—then bring him back here to the chapel."

I nodded.

"'Burn me up. Dump my ashes in the river. That way

nobody will ever find me.'" The nurse did a very good imitation of Mr. Kurz's raspy voice.

We both smiled. Suddenly the nurse ballooned and tilted as water welled up in my eyes.

The nurse put his hand on my shoulder. "You okay, kid?"

"Sure," I said quickly.

There was a pause. "I won't lie to you, Miles. It was sad. His family never even came for his ashes. And he never got around to telling me which river."

I blinked and blinked. Down the hall someone moaned loudly.

The nurse hesitated. Then he said, "Sorry. I gotta go. The living, you know."

"Sure. Thanks," I said. "See you around."

But he was already walking away toward the moaning.

BIRCH BAY

IN THE MORNING THE TENT was clammy and dewy inside.
Sarah—as usual—had managed to angle her sleeping
bag across most of the space. I quietly unzipped the tent
flap and looked outside. Our cabin was tall and still. For
a moment I hoped I had only dreamed the squatters—
but the Harley remained parked on the front porch.

I pulled on my shoes and slipped out. I'd always liked
early mornings down at the beach, before the lake got
busy with boats and whining little Jet Skis. I eased toward
the back side of the cabin (a nest of fresh cigarette butts
lay by the steps) and along its thick, reddish logs.

Our logs.

Our moss on our logs.

Our spiderwebs shiny with dew on our moss on our logs.

I suddenly felt ashamed to be sneaking along; I straightened up. I was almost down to the shore when the goats saw me. They began to lunge against their little corral fence and go *"Baack-baack-baack"* like crazy; I froze—and was still frozen when Danny the biker stumbled out the back door with a gun.

I knew a little bit about guns, mainly from Mr. Kurz, and this gun was huge. It was long, with a big barrel and a wooden forearm: a slide-action shotgun of some kind. Danny was jacking a shell into the chamber as he came out the back.

Then he saw me.

We stared at each other.

"What are you doing back here?" he growled.

"I'm going down to the beach."

"Why?"

I shrugged. I was usually fairly clever with words, but that gun shrank my vocal cords.

"I don't want you fooling around back here," Danny said. "You're making the goats nervous. They won't milk right."

Somehow I doubted that—the goats seemed more

like dogs that wanted to play—but I managed to say, "Sure, mister."

He stared at me, then lowered the gun. He nodded his head back toward our campsite and the *Princess*. "I meant to ask, what's the story on that buggy with the sail? I ain't ever seen one of those before."

"Probably not," I said.

"Your rich old man buy it somewhere?"

"No. I made it."

"You made it? No bull, kid?" Big Danny said.

"No bull."

"Pretty ding-danged impressive." He leaned the shotgun against the back porch and smiled like we were pals. "You're pretty handy for a scrawny little devil."

"Thanks," I said. My natural sense of sarcasm was coming back fast.

He stared at me for a long moment. "Too bad this cabin is full, else you folks could crash here for the winter. You'd be good around here, fixing things. Better than Rick, that's for sure. He's worthless with tools, and lazy besides."

I manufactured a weak smile. "I'm not that handy."

"Plus with five of them and four of you, there'd be one less mouth to feed." He cocked his head to consider that.

"Like I said," I quickly began, but he didn't hear me. Another idea had arrived, and clearly his brain could handle only one at a time.

"Except there's the sheriff." Then he added, "Plus Sheila would skin me alive."

"Well, there you have it, then."

He blinked, then bored his gaze back into me. "Listen. I got bad news. You tell your parents that you folks are gonna have to move on. That is, if they haven't already figured that out. There's no room here this winter for another family."

My throat stiffened. I stuck out my chin. "You're the big man around here—why don't you tell them?"

His face went blank, then broke into a gap-toothed grin. "You know, I like you, kid. I do."

I vamoosed back around the cabin and headed for the tent. My parents were up and around now. The food pack was out. They were debating whether to set up our cookstove. "It's a sign of defeat, us out here cooking, them inside," my mother said.

"On the other hand, we have to eat," my father said.

Sarah looked toward the cabin, then at the food.

We ate breakfast behind our tent, out of sight from the cabin. I didn't mention my conversation with Danny.

I kept staring at the ground, at our shoeprints in the ash. My brain was spinning. Processing. Searching all databases. We clearly needed a new plan. The whole family was silent as we ate bread, peanut butter, and jam. Midway, a woman's voice said, "Knock, knock."

Sheila poked her head around the side of the main tent.

My mother's face hardened. "What is it?"

"I brought you some coffee, if you like. Real coffee." She held two mugs.

My father glanced at Nat, then accepted a cup. My mother shook her head curtly sideways.

"I'll take it," I said. I surprised myself by saying that.

"I didn't know you drank coffee," Sarah said.

Sheila glanced briefly over her shoulder toward the cabin. "I wanted to invite you in for breakfast, but Danny said no. Says it would upset the children."

My mother bit her lower lip in a very obvious way. "Danny says," she repeated.

"Yeah, well, he is kind of the alpha male around here, if you know what I mean," Sheila replied.

"I'd noticed," my mother said.

"And I'm sorry to tell you this," Sheila said, lowering her voice, "but he's going to ask you to move on. I just wanted you to know that."

I looked at my father, and he at me.

"I'll talk with him after breakfast," my father said.

Sheila frowned. "I'm afraid there'll be nothing to talk about. Once his mind is made up, well, that's that."

"And what if we don't want to move on?" Sarah said suddenly. Her voice was high-pitched and shaky.

"Yes," my mother said, stepping close to Sarah. "What if we don't want to leave *our* own place, one that *we* pay taxes on, one that *we*—"

Sheila interrupted her. "Danny's been in prison," she said softly. "Deep down he's a good man, but he's done some bad things, and he's got a hair-trigger temper."

My father's gaze went to my mother. "That's good to know," he said.

Sarah looked accusingly at my father, as if he was on the wrong side.

"So I guess," Sheila said apologetically, "I'll leave you to make your plans."

When she had gone, we all looked at each other. My father's brown eyes went to the *Ali Princess*, then back to our cabin.

"Well, gang," he said cheerfully, "anybody got any ideas?"

"I say go back home. We should have never left," Sarah said, casting an accusing look my way.

I expected my mother to second that opinion, but she pursed her lips. "I was listening to the Minneapolis news last night. The Fresh Mart store in Wayzata was looted by a mob. The police shot and wounded two people."

"Wayzata?" Sarah said incredulously.

I thought of that "customer limits" sign.

"Plus there were several house break-ins and assaults in the west suburbs. A family of three was shot to death on Greenbriar Lane," she finished.

"My God!" Sarah said.

Greenbriar was only two miles from our house.

My father stepped forward. "It looks like there's a pattern developing. If you live in the suburbs and have a big house, then people think you must have stuff stashed away."

"It's the more isolated homes that are being hit," my mother said.

"That would be us," I muttered. I always knew our big house was trouble. Castles eventually attracted people with cannons and ladders; even I had read enough history to know that.

"What we're saying is that we can't go back," my

mother said to Sarah. "Your father and I won't put you children in that kind of danger."

At that moment Danny came around the corner of the tent.

"Good morning," my father said. More and more I admired my father's style with people. I had never seen that side of him.

Danny grunted.

"I've been thinking," my father said, stepping toward Danny. "Maybe there's another vacant cabin around here. Let's say we find a place, then we trade with you. We move in here like we ought to, and you move in someplace nearby."

"All well and good," said Danny. "But there ain't a vacant cabin for a hundred miles. I know: I've made the rounds on my bike. I've got friends in Milwaukee and Detroit who wanted to come. I told them to bring a tent if they do, and make it a mighty well insulated one, because you're going to be sleeping outside this winter."

No one said anything.

"Listen," Danny began, "I'm gonna put it to you straight: You folks are gonna have to move on. It's a dog-eat-dog world nowadays. Basically the deal is you got somewhere to go to and we don't."

My mother swallowed. "A family was killed last night just a few blocks from our home in Minneapolis."

Danny stared.

"That's what you're asking us to go back to."

Danny's gaze remained steady. "Tell you what. I'll give you a gun, teach you how to shoot it. That way you can defend yourselves. I'll give each of you a gun. Hell, one thing I got plenty of is guns," he said with a grin.

"Our family doesn't do guns," my mother said quietly.

Danny's smile faded. He looked at my father, who only shrugged. Nobody asked me.

"Well, don't say I didn't try to help you," Danny said angrily. He turned on his big boot heels and stalked away. At the porch steps he stopped and looked back to us. "You can camp here one more night," he yelled. "Then tomorrow I want you gone." Then he disappeared into the cabin. Our cabin.

Silence hung heavier than ever before.

"Well, gang, as I was saying, any ideas for our next gig?" my father said.

"You mean like where to be homeless?" Sarah asked. Her eyes were round with anger and fear.

My mind had already gone to the hard drive of my brain. To search mode. An idea—a crazy plan—hit me like a meteor exploding inside my skull. *Built it all myself, one log at a time. Plenty of trees around. Didn't cut them all from one spot, because the warden would spot me. Maybe from the river or else the air. He was always spying. Trying to find me. Trying to catch me. But I was too smart for him. Cut one tree here, one there, then rolled them downhill. That was the only way I could handle them, seeing as I didn't have a horse. Axe and a Swede saw and a block and tackle, that's all you need to build a place. It's not fancy, but it was mine.*

The idea was so far out that I clamped shut my lips. As a ninth grader I would have blurted it out, but not now. I needed to think more about it. And for it to work, everybody in my family needed to understand that we could not stay here at Birch Bay.

After breakfast I went over to a stump and sat where I could look out on Gull Lake. Then my gaze went to our cabin. *Made my own shingles. Plenty of white cedar in the swamp. Cut them in the winter when I could walk on the ice. One here, one there, sawed 'em in blocks, then split off shingles with my axe. Wood don't split well until it's twenty below zero. Then it cracks like glass. Roof hasn't leaked in sixty years. . . .*

Suddenly my father sat down nearby. "Sorry—didn't mean to startle you," he said.

"It's okay," I said.

We were silent.

He picked up a twig, spun it briefly around his fingers. "Well, Miles, what do you think?"

"About what?"

He smiled. "Our . . . predicament."

I shrugged. "In some ways, it's kind of my fault."

"How so?"

"I was the one who wanted to leave the city."

"And I was the one who wanted the big house," he replied.

We were silent.

"You know, sometimes I think if I hadn't seen that audition notice for Shawnee Kingston . . ."

I looked down, picked up a pebble.

"But I was teaching music to seventh graders. And it was killing me. All I ever wanted to do was play jazz, and there I was, stuck teaching scales."

I tossed my pebble hand to hand. This felt like a Talk, something we hadn't had for years.

"For me it was a question of either staying in my teaching job, and dying, or making a move to feel like I was living again," he continued.

I pitched the pebble hard into the water. "Yeah, but

did you think about us?" My voice was surprisingly sharp and loud.

He stared at the widening circles where my stone had hit. "I did. Believe me, I did," he said. "What if I made the band and was gone a lot? What would this do to my family? What would it do to my relationship with you?" He turned to me. "I thought of all those things."

I was silent. I was determined not to make this easy for him.

"But making the band seemed like a long shot at best," he continued. "So I took my sticks and went to the audition. I waited in line like everybody else. There were thirty or forty would-be drummers there, did you know that?"

"No," I said. I purposely didn't look at him.

"Anyway, each person was supposed to do five minutes—no more—of a Brubeck standard. So I got started. And we clicked. There's no other way to explain it. I found this rhythm. This groove. Jimmy and Carolyn and Shawnee kept playing and playing—probably fifteen minutes or more. I knew in my heart I was a good drummer, but this band—real musicians—brought it out in me. While we jammed, everything but the music went out of my head. When we finished, Shawnee and the others were laughing and clapping, and it was then I realized that I could give up anything—even my own family—for that kind of feeling."

I looked at him angrily.

His brown eyes were shiny and full. "It was the saddest moment of my life," he said. And walked away.

I sat there for a few minutes. I stared out at the water. Then I looked back at my family. They were sitting on the dusty grass and looking at their shoes. I got up and walked over to them. When none of them even glanced up at me, I understood this to be the lowest point ever in our family life.

"I have an idea," I said to them. "A place we can go."

SAVING MR. KURZ

AFTER THE NURSE TOLD ME about Mr. Kurz's death, I stood there in the hallway alone. I had the strange feeling that something in my life had tilted.

Shifted.

Spilled.

My next instinct was to get the hell out of Buena Vista. In a daze I headed down the hall, but somewhere I missed a turn. I thought the main door was just ahead, but suddenly I was walking through another wing of Buena Vista. More white-haired people, room after room of them. I walked faster. There were attendants in white uniforms here and there, but I didn't stop to ask my way. *I've never really been lost in the woods. I've been turned around for a couple of days, but never lost.*

Suddenly I arrived in a big open room with a high ceiling: the chapel. It was like a mini church built inside Buena Vista. Our family seldom went to church, especially after my father was gone, but now I stopped. More than anything, after the gleaming rat's maze of hallways it was the open space that felt good. Across, an old lady was playing the piano and a few quavery voices from wheelchair types were singing along. It was pathetic, but then again it kept them from looking at me. I sat down in a pew. I was actually slightly dizzy.

As I gathered my wits, the whole conversation with the nurse came back: *Bad news, Miles. . . . I won't lie to you. . . . His family never even came for his ashes. . . . He never got around to telling me which river. . . . Sorry. I gotta go. The living, you know. . . .*

The living. That was me. I looked up to the front of the chapel. I'm not much for religion, but at that moment my head cleared. Ideas have a kind of wind that blows away brain fog; suddenly I knew what needed to be done.

Retracing my steps, making the right turns this time,

I found Mr. Kurz's hallway. I went room to room until I found the nurse.

"Miles," he said with a puzzled look. He was cleaning a skinny old man's butt. The sight did not bother me a bit.

"Mr. Kurz's ashes," I said.

He looked at me. "Yes?"

"You said they're here?"

"That's right." He kept wiping.

"I know what river," I said.

A half smile came onto his face. "And?"

"And I'll scatter them," I said. "I'll do it. I want to do it."

He turned back to the pale, thin legs of the old man; he slipped on a diaper, then covered him with a blanket, tucking it tightly along the bed. He nodded his head toward the hallway, where we could talk.

"The paperwork says family," the nurse said. "Mr. Kurz's family."

"They didn't come," I said.

"Hey, it's a sad business, picking up an urn of ashes of a loved one. It's something that's easy to put off."

I shrugged. He started walking; I followed.

"Sometimes a family takes several months—even a

year—to come by for the clothes or whatever is left. We call them and call them. They say, 'We're so sad. We just can't *bear* to come.' Finally we say, 'There was a wallet— or a purse—some valuables that should be claimed.' Then they come right away."

I looked up.

"In other words, Miles, wait here," the nurse said. He smiled as he pointed. We had stopped by the storeroom—Mr. Kurz's room. I stepped inside. This time it didn't feel sad at all.

Within a couple of minutes the nurse ducked into the room carrying something wrapped in a white towel. He unwrapped a jar not much bigger than a maple syrup bottle. HANS R. KURZ was written on the side. "Here you go, Miles," he said.

I took the jar.

"What?" the nurse asked.

"I expected it to be heavier."

The nurse laughed. "No, we just get lighter and lighter as we get older. Pretty soon we hardly weigh anything at all." He glanced over his shoulder at the doorway.

"You won't get in trouble, will you? I mean, if his family comes for him and he's not here?"

The nurse grinned. "Hey, things get lost, misplaced,

misfiled—we do the best we can, right?"

"Thanks," I said.

"No problem."

There was a pause, and then—awkwardly—we shook hands.

"Don't drop him, Miles!" The nurse laughed. "Mr. Kurz wouldn't like that."

RETURN FAVOR

"MR. KURZ," I SAID TO my family. "He had a cabin."

My parents looked at me with puzzlement.

"Kurz? That crazy old guy from your memory book?" Sarah asked. At least she had read it.

I nodded.

"The one you always did imitations of?" Sarah added.

I shrugged.

"A cabin? Where?" my father asked. He stood up.

"Up north. Near the Mississippi headwaters. That's where he lived."

"Is he dead now?" my mother said.

"Yes," I said. I made sure my voice held steady. It was weird how I choked up when I thought about him. I turned away to dig out my Minnesota map.

"So one of his family probably has the place now," my mother said.

"I doubt that," I said with certainty. "He had some brothers and sisters, but they were all city types. His whole family didn't have much to do with one another. They all thought he was crazy."

"How did he end up in Minneapolis in a rest home?" my mother asked.

I explained about his sister's funeral. How his family trapped Mr. Kurz in the city. Put him in Buena Vista.

"That's sad," Sarah said.

My parents were silent.

"Well, certainly somebody must live in his cabin now," my mother said.

"Probably not," I said.

"Why?"

"There's no road to it. Though he did have a car," I added. *Didn't run on gasoline, it ran on itself.*

"How can you live in a cabin with no road to it but still have a car?" Sarah said.

I shrugged. "He said his road was the river." *Where I*

lived, a good man could jump clear across the Mississippi.

"Jump across the Mississippi!" Sarah said. "They were right. He was crazy."

I didn't realize I had spoken aloud. "He also said nobody ever bothered him there, not even the tax man."

"Not even the tax man?" my father repeated.

I nodded. "He was obsessed with not paying taxes."

"If you own land, you pay taxes," my mother said. "Nobody escapes real estate taxes."

The land belongs to the people. And I'm people. "He said he lived on public land," I replied.

My father's eyes blinked and blinked. He began to pace. "Maybe he had some kind of hunting shack on state-forest land. Lots of people do. There's thousands of acres of state land up north. If he did, and if you say nobody bothered him, then it certainly would be safe there."

My mother remained sitting. "Let's get serious. We need more than an imaginary cabin somewhere in the north woods."

"Yeah, Miles," Sarah added, though with less certainty than my mother. The "safe" part had caught her attention.

"Mr. Kurz *had* a cabin on the Mississippi. I know it,"

I said. "And I'll bet I could find it."

Everyone looked at me, then at our own cabin, and then back at me.

"And if you can't?" my mother said.

I shrugged. "Honestly?"

She nodded.

I met their gaze. "I don't know," I said quietly.

A crow cawed somewhere in the trees; in the silence it was as if our whole family life hung in the balance.

"How far away is this alleged cabin?" my mother said. She stood up. So did Sarah.

I had already opened my Minnesota map. I squinted down at it, then held my thumb against the mileage scale. "It's near Bemidji, which is up by the Mississippi headwaters. That's only about eighty miles. One day—or night—on the road."

My father looked toward the lake to check the waves. "The breeze is right," he said.

"Then some local exploring when we get there," I added. I tried not to be too enthusiastic, tried to hedge my bet just a bit; still, I knew the cabin was there. Mr. Kurz couldn't have made it *all* up.

"Well," my mother said uncertainly.

My father spoke up. "We know we can't go back

to the city—at least not yet. And for the moment we can't stay here. So if we go, what's the worst thing that can happen? We spend the summer camping on the Mississippi."

My mother was silent.

"Mr. Kurz said there was a freshwater spring near his cabin. There are probably fish in the river," I said.

"I still think it's a little crazy," she said. "But then so is the world right now."

"I hate that Danny," Sarah said, shooting a look toward Birch Bay. "Anyplace would be better than here."

With sudden energy we set about packing. It was exciting, as if we were striking out on a family trip—the best kind of trip—one with no exact destination. As I finished stuffing our sleeping bags and stowing my gear (I'm a fast packer), I heard the sound of someone splitting wood down by the lake.

"I'll be back in a minute," I said.

When I came around the corner of the cabin, the goats went crazy again. Big Danny looked up from beside a woodpile. He was sweating, and with the axe in hand he looked like Paul Bunyan.

"What do you want, kid? Don't tell me they sent you

to get me to change my mind."

"No. We're leaving," I said.

"So you came to say good-bye, then." He grinned.

"Not really," I said. "I came for a gun."

PACKING

HE LOOKED AT ME. "A gun," he repeated.

"You offered my family a gun. And I accept."

He pursed his lips. His eyes scanned me up and down. I thought he was going to say something about my age, or my size. But he didn't.

"If I give you a gun, you ain't going to shoot me with it?"

"No," I said (not that I hadn't thought about it). "It's not for people. Unless, I don't know, if I had to sometime . . ." That last part slipped out. I thought of those losers under the bridge, their cigarette smoke. I thought of those bandits on their four-wheelers.

"That's exactly right, kid," Danny said. He turned, tossed his axe overhand at the nearest tree; after two rotations the axe flashed and went *chonk*, blade first, into the bark. I was impressed. "A family like yours, from the city and all," he said, taking off his gloves, "if you're gonna make it through these times, you might have to do things you never done before."

"I mainly want the gun for food," I said. "If we run out and can't buy any, I can hunt."

"You ever hunted before?"

"Nope."

"But you're a fast learner," he said.

I nodded.

He grinned, gap-toothed. "Anyway, nobody can teach nobody how to hunt. You got to learn the woods on your own. So first things first: What do you know about guns?"

"I've heard a few things," I said, meaning stories from Mr. Kurz. I didn't want to go into that here. "And I've shot a BB gun a few times."

"That's it? That's all? Your family never had a gun of any kind?"

I shrugged. "No."

He shook his head sadly. "Parents like yours ought to be arrested. Well, luckily school is in session, kid. Wait here."

Soon he returned from the cabin carrying a heavy duffel bag with both hands. Steel clanked inside it. He opened a padlock around the handles. He started laying out weapons large and small, long and short.

"Geez!" I said without meaning to.

"Don't ask where these come from. That ain't important anyway. I'll just say that a gun is made to be shot, not hung on somebody's wall." It looked to me like he had knocked off about fifty walls somewhere.

"Let's see, here's a thirty aught six—that's a deer rifle—but this one will knock you on your can. . . .

"Here's a twelve-gauge shotgun, pump, but it's a little long for you. . . .

"Here's a nice lightweight twenty-two pump action, accurate but mainly a squirrel gun. Not enough stopping power, if you dig. . . ."

I swallowed and nodded once.

"This one's a nine-millimeter semiautomatic, but a pistol's not a good beginner's gun, no way, and it's no good for hunting. . . ."

He stood up and looked me over and stroked his

beard. "We need something just right. . . . Wait a minute." He dug deeper in the bag and came out with a medium-sized long gun with a bolt action. "Bingo!" he said.

He handed it to me. I put it to my shoulder.

"Whoa!" he said angrily, hopping sideways. "First thing you gotta learn is muzzle safety." He batted the barrel end away from him toward the lake. "You never point the muzzle at somebody unless you mean to use it—got that?"

"Sorry," I said.

"Consider any gun loaded until you know it ain't. If you do that, nobody ever gets shot even if you were an idiot and the gun did go off by accident."

That made sense.

"What you're holding there is a four ten shotgun."

"It looks like a rifle," I said. It had a skinny barrel like a rifle.

"Small-bore shotguns are kinda in between," Danny said. "The four ten number means that the barrel diameter is just a hair over four tenths of an inch. Lots of guns are named that way—for the size of their bore."

"How many shells does it hold?"

"Just one. And one's enough for a scrawny little devil like you."

I shrugged. I was thinking more along the lines of something I could jack shells into while riding the *Princess*, like Arnold Schwarzenegger did on his Harley in those old *Terminator* flicks.

He dug in the bag and produced a box of shells, then tossed a single to me. It was a tube of hard red plastic seated in a small brass cup. The shell was about the same length and diameter as my pointer finger. The plastic end was crimped inward; the whole thing had a faint rattle.

"That's fine shot you hear," Danny said. "Tiny steel balls a little bigger than coarse sand, a little smaller than BBs."

I nodded.

"You can buy shotgun shells with different shot size, all the way from a real fine shot like number nine, which is almost like salt, on down through six, and four, and coarser—the smaller the number, the bigger and fewer the shot. The last stop on that chart is a slug."

"A slug?"

He looked at me. "You really are stupid, aren't you? But it ain't your fault. It's how you was raised." He dug deeper and found a few loose shells. He examined the ends, then tossed one to me. I could see solid, dark lead poking out from the crimped end.

"That there's a single chunk of lead, one per shell."

"Like a rifle bullet," I said.

"You got it, kid. And the slug, well, that's the beauty about this four ten. You could kill a deer or a bear with this—or let the air out of someone coming after that pretty sister of yours." He grinned at me.

I kept my face blank. Now, for sure, if there was anyone I could imagine shooting, it was Danny.

"On the other hand, you can shoot ducks and grouse—on the fly—just by switching to fine shot."

I looked at my gun.

"Ready to try it?"

I swallowed. "Okay."

He glanced around, found a beer bottle, and pitched it out in the water. The bottle splashed, then began to bob along with its thin neck up.

"Here's how the bolt works." He stood close beside me (his T-shirt smelled like vinegar; his breath was worse). "Lift up, pull back; shell in; push forward, then down. Now you're locked and loaded."

Squinting my eyes against his smell, I dropped in the shell and followed directions.

"Take aim on that bottle."

I sighted down the barrel; my heart was pounding. The muzzle bobbed and weaved more than the waves.

"Squeeze it off."

I pressed the trigger—harder and harder—but nothing happened. I jerked at it; still nothing.

Danny laughed. "You know why it didn't shoot?" he said.

I shook my head sideways.

"Because the safety was on. I did that on purpose." His stench washed over me again as he leaned close. He put his finger on a little lever just behind the bolt. "'S' and 'F.' That means 'safe' and 'fire.' It's one more way to keep your gun from firing accidentally. They may be in different locations, but all guns got some kind of safety."

"I see."

"You ready now?"

"Yes."

"Okay. Lever to 'F.'"

I clicked it sideways.

"Squeeze—and don't flinch this time—it ain't gonna hurt you."

Suddenly the gun bucked against my shoulder and cheek and the bottle sprayed into brilliant bits of glass. "Hey, Daniel Boone himself," Danny said.

Except that within seconds Daniel Boone's whole family came racing around the corner of the cabin. "Miles?" my father cried, running just ahead of my mother.

They drew up when they saw me holding the gun.

"What are you *doing*?" my mother said. The fear in her voice turned instantly to anger. She glared at Danny.

"It's all right," my father said to her.

"He's getting a lesson in how to use his new gun," Danny replied.

"*His* new gun?" my mother asked.

"If you recall, I offered your family one. Your boy here took me up on it," Danny said with a shrug.

"We are not taking a gun," my mother began.

Danny stared. He spit to the side. "I guess it goes to show that there's all different kinds of child neglect."

"What do you mean by that?" my mother shot back.

Danny pointed and glared. "Your kind of parent annoys the hell out of me. You raise your kids on public television and nature shows. Then when the going gets tough—like nowadays—you won't pick up a gun if your life depended on it. Well I'm telling you right now it might. The highway out there is full of dudes way badder than me. And if you're not going to protect your kids, you might as well leave them here. We'd at least try to take care of them."

"Yeah, right," Sarah whispered.

"Who the hell do you think you are?" my mother replied, her eyes fixed on Danny. "What gives you the right to judge us as parents?"

"Nat, easy," my father said. He put a restraining hand on her arm. He looked at me. "Do you know how to use that?" He pointed to my gun.

I nodded.

"He can handle it," Danny agreed. "The kid's all right."

"Okay. Then he can have it," my father said. "And I'll take one too."

I turned quickly to my father. My mother's jaw slipped open. For once in her life she was speechless.

"Hey, there's plenty of firepower for everybody," Danny said.

My mother's mouth moved but no words came out. "Come on, Mother," Sarah said, tugging at her arm. With Sarah moving her along, they headed back toward the tent.

My father knelt down and peered uncertainly into the bag of weapons.

"Hang on just a second," Danny said to him. "I gotta show your boy how to break down his gun. Then we'll find one for you."

I watched him unscrew a nut on the forearm, then separate the barrel from the stock. "Easier to conceal this way, too," he said with a wink, "plus it looks less scary for your ma." He handed me the two pieces, then two boxes of shells.

Something in me would not let me thank him, but he seemed to understand that.

"I got something a little heavier duty for you," Danny said to my father.

"How about something medium duty?" he replied.

Danny chuckled. "If you can handle drumsticks, you can handle this sweet little slide-action twenty gauge."

I was jealous already.

Danny showed him the mechanism and the safety button, and then tossed a bottle for my father. He drew up and missed it cleanly—but only by a couple of feet. Water sprayed.

"Again," Danny said.

This time the bottle exploded.

"Right on," Danny said. "You guys ain't half bad shots." He dug out a box of shells and handed them over.

Then it was just the three us, my father and I holding guns, and Danny empty-handed.

Danny's gaze flickered down to our guns. He realized his situation, and grinned. "I guess I never was an A student."

"Well, consider it your lucky day, then," my father said. "The Newell family doesn't have a long history of shooting people. Though maybe by the time we come back here, we'll have learned." There was a hardness, an edge to his voice that surprised me.

Danny's grin flattened. "You know, I don't doubt that."

"And count on it—we will be back," my father said. He turned my way. "Let's go, Miles."

Danny's wife, Sheila, had been watching from the porch the whole time. As we passed, she called to me, "Tell your sister I've got something for her, too." She glanced toward Danny, who suddenly seemed more fat than big and strong. "A little gift for the road."

Back by the *Princess*, which was now nearly loaded, I found Sarah. "Danny's wife has a free parting gift for you," I said. It was an inside joke with us; we had always thought that the saddest phrase in the world was *free parting gift*.

Puzzled, wary, Sarah walked to the cabin while I lashed down the gear and inspected the *Princess*. I kept an eye out and saw her go with Sheila down toward the lake, out of sight.

Five minutes passed. "I'll go see what's going on," my father said. He took along his gun. But he had taken only a few steps when Sarah rounded the corner of the cabin. She had a stunned, blank look on her face. Attached to her hand was a small rope. Attached to the rope was a small brown goat.

"This is Emily," Sarah said. "Emily now belongs to us."

CHAPTER
FIFTEEN

HEADING NORTH

A FAMILY LIKE YOURS, FROM *the city and all, if you're gonna make it through these times, you might have to do things you never done before. . . .*

We left Birch Bay with Emily, a crossbreed Alpine goat, trotting along on her rope behind the *Ali Princess*. Trotting for all of ten feet. Then she hit the skids. Dug in with four pointy little hooves. Wouldn't budge. She kept staring at us with her weird frog eyes—two bumps way up high and out to the sides of her head—and going *"Baack, baack!"*

"We're not going 'baack'—at least for now!" Sarah

said with exasperation. "Either come along or Miles will drag you."

"I will?"

Suddenly Emily hopped on board—and scrambled high atop the luggage. There she perched like a carved figure on the bow of an old ship.

"Good work, Goat Girl!" I said.

"I'm not Goat Girl!" Sarah yelled.

"Hey, Emily belongs to you," I replied.

As we pedaled the *Princess* down the bumpy gravel driveway, Emily kept her balance and her nose forward like a sailor scanning the ocean. Like she'd been doing this for years.

"Baack!" she said occasionally, though she clearly preferred going forward. When we reached the hard asphalt of the highway, my father prepared to run up the sail. Emily went *"Baack! Baack!"* excitedly.

"You don't get out much, is that it?" Nat muttered to Emily. So far my mother had kept a maximum distance from the goat.

"She's clearly a road goat," I said.

"Born to ride," Sarah added.

Our mood was weird—light and joky. We'd just had our cabin stolen by squatters and bikers. We were reduced to heading down the dusty highway like Okies in the Great Depression. But no one was arguing or complaining. It was a miracle.

"Why do we have Emily, again?" my mother asked.

"She's a milking goat," Sarah said; she looked to me, but I held up both hands defensively—as did Mom and Dad.

"I'll bet Sheila showed you how to milk her, right, Goat Girl?"

Sarah glared at me but wouldn't answer.

"See," I said triumphantly. "You do know how to milk her."

"What if no one milks her?" my mother asked.

"She dries up," Sarah said.

"And blows away?" I added. Stupid joke.

"No, she soon quits making milk. At least I think." Sarah took out a sheet of paper; there was a list of notes in Sheila's handwriting.

"Emily's instruction manual," I said.

My father smiled; even my mother grinned.

"Not funny, Miles!" Sarah said.

"Baack!" went Emily.

So with goat and guns on board, the *Princess* caught a quartering south breeze and began to roll north. I wasn't fond of traveling in daylight, but the wind was perfect. And now we had weapons.

I touched the cold hard barrel of my shotgun. One part of me was excited by having my own gun. Another part of me understood this was not a toy—that packing a gun meant a lot of things in life had gone bad. A gun could probably make them worse—way worse—in a flash. I glanced at my father. He, too, was looking down at his gun.

The highway was pale with dust, and the pine forest shaggy white on either side. There were no tracks in the ash other than those of animals, probably deer and coyotes. The lakes were smaller now, and slightly bluer than those in central Minnesota. "Hole in the Day Lake," Sarah observed, pointing to a green highway sign. "What a great name."

"The Hole in the Head Family?" my mother said, giving Emily a glance.

As we rolled along smoothly north, the town names began to sound more Indian: Nisswa, Pequot. After a long stretch of farmland and very smooth sailing, we entered some hilly country that required us all to pedal. All except Miss Emily.

We turned by a casino that, weirdly, was very busy.

Buses came and went; little white-haired people peered at us from behind the tinted glass of their dusty coaches. Emily went *"Baack!"* at the buses and the bright flashing marquee lights.

"You don't want to go there," Nat said to Emily. "Gambling is a bad habit."

Ah-Gwah-Ching, then the town of Walker, which lay on the south side of some major water called Leech Lake. We stopped at a Dairy Queen there, which had ridiculously high prices but normal-sized portions of ice cream. At least nobody so far seemed paranoid about "strangers." In fact I think the brown-eyed girl behind the counter kind of liked me.

"Cool wheels," she said of the *Princess.*

"Thank you," I said. The girl and I smiled at each other. She looked to be a senior in high school, maybe even older than that.

"He made it," Sarah said, smiling at the girl.

I can't tell you how I hated Sarah when she did that.

"Really?" the girl said; she gave me an admiring look.

"He's very clever for being sixteen," Sarah added.

I kneed her, out of sight below the counter.

"Is that, like, a goat?" the girl said, changing the subject; clearly I was too young for her.

"Yes. She belongs to my sister, Goat Girl," I replied.

Sarah gave me her I'll-get-you-later-big-time-for-this look.

"Do goats like ice cream?" the brown-eyed girl asked. "I messed up an order that's just going to be thrown out."

I glanced at Sarah, who turned to Emily. *"Baack!"* went Emily.

The girl filled a paper cup with melted vanilla ice cream. At the sight of it in Sarah's hand, Emily bounded down from her perch and mashed her nose directly into the mush. A blob formed on her nose as she lapped and lapped at the cup. She made happy, bubbling sounds. "I'd say she eats ice cream," Sarah observed.

"So where you guys going?" the girl said, looking again at the *Princess*. A small group of locals had gathered to look at our "wheels," including several motocross-type riders. Their engines barked as they showed off wheel stands.

"Ah . . . up north," I said lamely. I kept my eyes on the motocross riders. I wanted to tell her everything, but I had a sudden flash of that carp in shallow water; of his fin sticking out. Weird how I couldn't get that image out of my mind.

"You have friends or someplace to stay?"

"Oh yes," I said easily, with a sideways glance to my family.

"That's good," the brown-eyed girl said.

"Why? Aren't there places around here?" my mother asked casually.

"No way!" the girl said. "Everything's full, and there are more and more of these icky homeless people around now." Her eyes returned to the *Princess* and fell for the first time upon our luggage. Her face colored slightly. "If you know what I mean," she said.

"Oh definitely," Sarah said, "I just hate icky homeless people, don't you, Miles?"

"Time to go," my mother said cheerfully.

I agreed. There were a few too many gawkers for my taste.

We boarded, me at the handlebars now, and pedaled down Main Street.

"Icky homeless people," Sarah repeated. "I wish Emily would have bit her fingers off."

"But we're glad Emily didn't," my mother said, giving the goat a wary look.

I glanced back over my shoulder toward the Dairy Queen. I kept thinking what a nice round face and brown eyes the girl had. And round other parts, too. She had made me dizzy when I looked straight at her.

"Miles—steady as she goes!" my father said. A small motorcycle came straight at us, then veered north, out of sight.

"He's thinking of you-know-who," Sarah said.

I glared at her.

"Told you so," Sarah said.

I hated it when people in my family read my mind.

"He hates when I read his mind," Sarah said.

"Shut up!" I shouted.

"All right, that's enough," my mother said.

Families: they'll drive you crazy. On the other hand, it took all four of us, pedaling hard, to make it up the long slope of the highway north of town. And because I couldn't get the girl out of my head, I forgot to watch our back.

A mile beyond town, where the road curved into the trees, a dozen chain saws fired up in the woods.

"Miles! Here they come!" my father yelled.

From both sides of the highway, soaring over embankments and up the shoulders, raced the motocross riders. It was like we had fallen into a motorcycle race or a state-fair thrill show. In a chaos of dust and noise, they began to box us in.

"Lock and load," I shouted to my father.

"Aim low!" he yelled back.

A leader, in black leather, black helmet, and visor, drew a pistol and waved it at us. My father, in the right rear bay, stood up and fired. The leader's rear wheel exploded in shreds of rubber and wire spokes; the bike pitched forward and ejected its rider into the ditch, where he tumbled like roadkill.

I swung and squeezed—and blew out the rear tire of another bike. It, too, flopped over—exactly in the path of another bandit, who *thump-thumped* over the rider. Suddenly the chain saws were gone, receding back up the embankments. The two dumped riders, scrabbling like insects, crawled after them and disappeared into the brush.

My mother and Sarah, heads low, hands over their ears, kept pedaling at high speed. My father and I stared at each other.

"You all right?" he asked.

I nodded.

"You look kind of white," he said.

I laughed once. Sort of a single, strange bark of a laugh.

"You didn't kill anybody, did you?" Sarah breathed. She risked a look back.

"No, we didn't kill anybody," I said. "A couple of motorcycles, maybe."

My father laughed, and we high-fived each other.

"I can't believe I hit that tire," he said.

"Me neither," I said. "I aimed for the front and hit the rear!"

Adrenaline pumped through me. I held my gun aloft. "So," I said to my mother. "Our family doesn't do guns?"

She looked at me, then at my father.

"I hate these times," she said softly. She turned away as if she couldn't bear to look at us right now.

FARTHER NORTH

LATER THAT AFTERNOON WE WERE dragging, particularly my father and I. The adrenaline rush of scaring off the motocrooks was gone. Into its place had trickled a strangely depressed feeling—at least I felt it, but I could sense it in my father, too. Right after the encounter, we had whooped and held up our guns like big-time terminators. Now we were quiet.

The wind was switching too.

"There's a campground not far ahead in the Chippewa National Forest," I said, checking the map. We were about fifteen miles east of Bemidji, and no more than twenty-five or so from Kurz's cabin. Alleged cabin, as my mother would have said.

"I'm ready," my father breathed.

The entrance to Norway Beach Campground curved between tall, thick pine trees, and led to big Lake Winnibigoshish somewhere beyond. There were several sets of footprints—adults' and children's—on the narrow, ashy road. Even Sarah noticed the tracks. Just to be safe, my mother put on "the vest," and then we pedaled forward between the trees.

As we came around the last curve before the lake, a gate blocked the road. It was crudely made—somebody was a real wood butcher here—from thin boards and bent-over nails. But a gate was a gate. And a guard was a guard. A burly woman with a shotgun slung over her shoulder stepped from behind the trees.

"I thought I'd seen it all," she said. She blocked the middle of the road as she stared at the *Princess*.

"Good afternoon," my mother said.

The woman nodded, then looked up. "You're not looking to camp here?"

"Are you a park ranger?" my mother replied.

"In a manner of speaking," the woman said. She had beefy arms and big hands. Her eyes flickered down my mother's body.

"I ask because this is a national park, right?" Nat said.

"Right," the guard said. "But these days, well, the real rangers are not around much. So it's first come, first served. And as you can see, we here in the campground are first come." Behind her, through the trees, I could see dense clusters of motor homes, trailers, and tents, plus patches of gray-blue water beyond.

"Are you saying you're full?" my mother asked.

"That's what I'm saying."

"We're just looking for one night," my mother said easily. "Be on our way first thing in the morning."

The guard glanced at Nat; at her big belly. "Looks like you folks gonna have another mouth to feed pretty soon."

"That's right," my mother said. "Another three months or so."

The guard shrugged. "Okay, one night then. As long as we're clear on that."

"We're clear," my father said. His voice sounded tired and flat.

"Then that will be a hundred for the one night."

"A hundred?" Mother asked.

"Dollars," the woman said. "Cash."

"For who?" Mother exclaimed. "Who gets the hundred?"

"Campground management," the woman said. "Mainly security, night watchmen, that sort of thing. Sometimes we have to weed out undesirables. People who don't fit in, if you know what I mean."

"Of course," my mother said, barely keeping her sarcasm in check.

The guard hoisted the gate to one side. "Head over to the far right. Temporary camping. And keep that goat close or else the wild dogs will get her."

Sarah's eyes widened. We pedaled forward.

"Another mouth to feed," Nat muttered after we cleared the gate.

"Hey, nice work again, Mom," I said to her.

She turned to Sarah. "If I'm six months along, that means I'm carrying this for three more months. After that, you're going to start wearing the vest."

Sarah's eyes widened. "No way!" she said. "I'm too young."

"Don't ever say that," my mother said.

An audience of raggedy kids quickly gathered to stare at us and the *Ali Princess*. They watched as we set up tents close alongside the *Princess*. None of them said anything. I leaned my shotgun where everyone passing could see it.

"It's like we're in a Charles Dickens novel," my mother said.

"Or *Lord of the Flies*," Sarah replied.

When the world got back to normal, I really did plan to read more.

Two boys, carrying sharp little sticks in their belts, pointed at Emily and grinned at each other. They eased forward, almost within touching distance of the family goat—until Sarah saw them.

"She bites!" Sarah said loudly. The boys jumped back; the other kids laughed at them, and then all of them raced off shouting and chasing.

"I guess they're just kids," my mother said.

I hoped so. What worried me was their parents. Eyes peeped from other sagging tents and dusty vehicles. The other campers were well settled under tarps and ropes and layers of dust; some had crude swing sets; most of the vehicles had flat tires, and makeshift curtains inside. One big, dusty Chevy Suburban had a hole cut in the top where a small chimney poked through.

"The long-term camping section," my father observed.

"No kidding," I replied.

My father, too, kept his gun nearby.

As I worked, I saw Sarah, carrying a plastic bucket, leading Emily behind the *Ali Princess*. The gang of little kids was back; they went with Sarah.

"Where are you going?" I asked.

"Shut up, Miles," Sarah said. She ignored the little kids.

"Finish the tent and mind your own business, Miles," my mother said.

"Sure," I said, grinning at Sarah. My sister, milking a goat: Someday I would get a picture of this and make sure it got into her high school yearbook.

A few minutes later the tents were done, and so was Emily. Sarah came back carrying a nearly full pail, and Emily, on a short rope, grazed and nibbled at the dusty grass.

"So what do I do with this?" Sarah said; she held up the bucket.

"Warm goat's milk—great!" I said.

My father scratched his beard stubble. "Miles, do we have any extra containers? Something with a lid?" He looked at me.

For an instant I thought he knew—but that was stupid. "One of the water jugs is empty," I said.

"That will work. Let's pour the milk in there, make

sure it's sealed tight, and then we'll put it in the lake."

"It'll drift away," my mother said.

"We'll find a stone and string and keep it submerged."

While Mother watched the campsite, the three of us went down to the lake. We made sure we could see the *Ali Princess* from the shore.

Sarah splashed in first, then dove under. "It's really cold just a few feet down!" Sarah said, gasping as she surfaced. She was a good swimmer. I also noticed that her body actually had some curves. Amazing! Disgusting, kind of. The thought of my little sister someday having a woman's body simply did not add up in my head.

I put a toe in the water. "Yikes!" No way I was going in. I watched, shivering, as Sarah and my father then secured the goat's milk about six feet down, and out of reach of the little kids. They were both good swimmers, and I was impressed: my father and sister actually figuring out how to do something. Maybe there was hope for us after all.

"Aren't you coming in, Miles?" Sarah teased.

"It's too cold!" I called.

"You could use a bath," she said.

I shrugged. "No. I'm fine."

"I hate to say this, Miles, but she's right," my father said. "You are getting a little rank." He tossed me a bar of soap.

When I took the plunge, I think I shouted underwater. I never believed water could get this cold without becoming ice. Within a minute I was washed, dried, and back shivering by the tents.

"Well, look at you!" my mother said. "You look like a drowned rat—but a clean drowned rat."

"Thanks," I said. "You should go for a swim, Mother. Really—the water's very nice."

"And what do I do with the baby?" she said, hefting her vest.

"Sorry. I forgot." I really had.

"Don't worry, I'll slip down later and wash up a bit."

That night Emily kept us up late crying just outside our tent—I swear she sounded like a real baby.

"She's not used to a short rope," Sarah said.

"Whatever you say, Goat Girl," I mumbled, and finally drifted off to sleep.

I slept lightly until, much later, I heard a stick snap.

Then silence; someone had paused outside the tent. Sarah snoozed on. Slowly I rolled over and touched the shotgun. It was empty. Then I heard boots—more than two of them—come closer.

I jacked the bolt open and shut on my shotgun. Sticks crackled as boots thudded away.

"What!" Sarah said, waking up confused.

"Nothing," I said, lowering the shotgun so she didn't see it. "It's okay."

"Emily?"

"She's fine. Go to sleep." Sarah collapsed back onto her pillow and was breathing softly again within thirty seconds. I lay where I could look out the tent flap. For good measure I poked the gun barrel a few inches into the night. Moonlight glinted on its steel. I imagined the single dark eye of its muzzle staring out from our tent. With it on guard, gradually I let my eyes close.

In the morning birds chirped. For once there was no radio muttering the usual bad news. I also realized I was alone in the tent. As I crawled out into sunlight, Sarah handed me a large, steaming mug of hot chocolate. I blinked and rubbed my face. I had slept late. And Sarah, up before me? Handing me hot chocolate? There was a good chance I was dreaming.

The hot chocolate tasted a little odd—kind of thick and woody.

"See—I knew he'd try it!" Sarah began to laugh wildly, and Emily went *"Baaack!"*

I looked at the mug.

I looked at Emily.

"Goat's milk cocoa." Sarah grinned.

My parents and Sarah—how nice of them—were waiting for my verdict before they filled their mugs.

"Mmmm, tasty," I said, holding back a slight gagging sensation as I took another long sip. As Sarah and Mother made breakfast, I inspected the footprints in the ash. The close-together tracks; the sudden running strides. And the little dry sticks on the ground all around our tent. I didn't remember these sticks from the night before.

My father joined me. "We had visitors last night," he said.

"Yeah," I said. "I heard them. One of them stepped on the sticks." The sticks that had me puzzled.

My father looked back at Mother and Sarah at the campfire. They were talking to some little raggedy kids and giving them some of the leftover hot chocolate.

"Do you remember the *Godfather* movie, the first one?"

"Sure," I said. He and I used to have *Godfather* movie

sessions; once we stayed up all night and watched all five in a row.

"There's a line when Don Corleone says, 'Women and children can afford to be careless, but men can't,'" he said.

I nodded.

"It's sort of a lame speech. But I thought of it last night. So after dark I got up and put those twigs around our tents."

I looked at him. I swear he was a foot taller than when we left the city.

At that moment a couple of gaunt, dusty guys in caps wandered over as if to check on the children. "You folks have a good night's sleep?" the taller man asked.

"Just fine. You?" my father asked.

"Sure thing," he said.

There was silence.

"So you folks moving on today?"

"That's right," my father said.

"Whereabouts you headed?" the taller one said pleasantly. He smiled as if passing the time of day.

"North," I said suddenly. "Heading up to Canada."

My father looked at me suddenly, then regained a poker face.

The two men glanced at the *Ali Princess*, then back at us. "Well, have a nice trip," they said.

"Thanks a lot," I said.

When they had gone, my father said quickly, "Why did you tell them we're heading north?"

"Because they're no fools," I said.

He looked at me.

When we pedaled—thankfully—away from the campground from hell, we first turned south onto the dusty highway. Our tires left narrow lines in the pale ash. But a hundred yards or so down the road, we pulled the *Ali Princess* off the highway and into the trees. With a pine branch I fluffed away our tracks on the shoulder and in the ditch. Then we hid ourselves out of sight but with a view of the road. My father and I kept our shotguns handy.

Barely ten minutes passed before a group of six men, all on mountain bikes and all carrying guns strapped across their backs, came up the campground driveway. They paused at the highway and looked down to the dust.

"South," one of them called. "I told you they'd lie. You can't be that dumb and make it this far."

"Let's get after them," another said.

The posse of bikers sped south after our faded, disappearing tracks.

We pedaled into Bemidji at noon, happy to be out of the forest and off lonely Highway 2. In Bemidji we once again crossed the Mississippi River. Its waters slid under a low bridge no wider than a tennis court, then entered the south end of Lake Bemidji. The big lake stretched northward almost out of sight. My map showed the river leaving the far end of the lake.

Across the bridge, at lakeside, was a dusty, silent amusement park complete with big statues of Paul Bunyan and Babe the Blue Ox. Like normal tourists, we pulled in for a look at the statues. There was a tourist information building just beyond, with a sign that read OPEN. We went inside.

A young woman at the counter lowered her *Teen* magazine; she looked at us like we were ghosts. Or aliens. Or the first tourists she had seen all summer. She cleared her throat. "May I help you?"

"Got any brochures and local maps?" I said.

"Sure, sure, all kinds of them," she said, and started to lay some out on the counter.

I looked through them. "Any that show state land?"

"You mean like public land? If you want to hunt or something?"

"Exactly," I said.

Behind her, from deeper in the office, an older, unsmiling woman appeared.

"You're looking for?" the older woman asked.

"We're not sure. We're on vacation," my mother said easily. Outside, Emily went *"Baaack!"*

"The resorts here are full, sorry," the older woman said, "and so are all other accommodations." She didn't look at all sorry.

"Then why are you open for tourists?" Nat asked with her cheerful but steady gaze.

The young woman at the counter looked away with embarrassment; I seized the opportunity to stuff my shirt with maps of all kinds, particularly the one showing public land.

"I'm just following the mayor's orders," the older woman said, her face flushing. "We're not to encourage people to stay here."

"Well, congratulations, you've done your job," Nat said.

I shrugged apologetically at the young woman and then followed my family out the door.

"Now what?" Sarah said. We looked up at giant Paul Bunyan and his towering blue ox. They stared blankly west.

"The maps," I said dramatically, holding up a whole sheaf.

We sat along the shore. They ate lunch as I pored over the maps. "Did you notice that the Mississippi flows north here?"

"No, I didn't," Sarah said sarcastically.

"There's a continental divide not far from here," I observed. "I mean, like, what if the Mississippi didn't turn south but instead kept going north into Canada?"

"Well, we wouldn't have Tom Sawyer and Huck Finn," my mother said, always the literary person.

"There you have it," I said.

I love those kinds of questions. I especially liked to bring them up in history class. "Like, what if Germany instead of America had developed the first atomic bomb?" "Like, what if Kennedy had not been assassinated?"

Like, what if the Cascade Mountain range had not vaporized itself? . . .

I glanced at my road-warrior family. Already we were looking shabby and dusty again. It would be nice to find "home" soon. I leaned closer and began to trace the Mississippi River as it flowed through state-forest land.

Downstream from the Iron Bridge. That's all I'll say.

"There!" I said.

My father leaned in to look.

"There's a triangle of state land cut off from the road," I said. "That has to be it."

My father nodded.

"We follow Fifth Street west, then take County Road 11 down to 7," I said. I liked the lucky numbers. "That will take us mostly along the Mississippi, though we probably won't be able to see it because it's a ways back in the forest."

My father leaned in to look. "And Kurz's cabin?"

"I remember him mentioning the Iron Bridge west of town, which must be here." I moved my finger on the map.

"And from there?" my father asked.

"Downstream. That I know for sure."

"Come on, Memory Boy, you'll have to do better than that," Sarah said.

"I'll find it. We're not far, just a few miles," I said. Nothing could bring down my mood; I felt like a real explorer, like Lewis and Clark combined.

"Well, I'm just glad that we aren't heading into the mountains and our name isn't Donner," Sarah said.

We passed through Bemidji, a nice-enough-looking small town that even had a state university stretched out on the lakeshore. (I could see going to college in a location like that; maybe that's where brown-eyed Dairy Queen girls went to college.) Then we headed west and south on a narrow tar road. No sign of the Mississippi. But I could tell from the curving road that it was not far beyond the trees. We passed a ramshackle place that advertised RIVER TUBEING. Not only was their sign misspelled, it was falling down.

A few miles south and west of town, the *Princess* began to roll more freely, then coast without being pedaled; we headed into a long, downhill curve.

"The Iron Bridge," I called, and pointed. "That has to be it."

"Aren't all bridges made out of iron?" Sarah said.

We rolled to a stop. The river here was less than a tennis court wide, and its flow lazy and shallow and clear. Underwater grass waved slowly downstream, where the river disappeared into marshland.

"Well, Memory Boy, where do we go from here?" Sarah said.

"Shut up, Goat Girl," I said as I spread out the maps.

"That's enough," Mother said. My father leaned in to study the maps. "We're just inside the Mississippi Headwaters State Forest," he said.

"So?" Sarah said.

I looked up. South and east, beyond the marshland, low hills and forest rose up. "So Mr. Kurz's cabin is just down there," I said.

"Great," Sarah said. "So how do we get there?"

I looked down at the water; it was waist deep, clear and steady in its flow.

The river was my road. . . .

"Easy. We just need a boat," I said.

QUARTER TWAIN

AFTER THE *ALI PRINCESS*, THE *Princess River Queen* was my next-most-impressive invention. She had required only four hours to make, half of which was taken up by transporting three large truck-tire inner tubes down the highway to the Iron Bridge. The river-rafting guy ("Tubeing") was a loser and happy to sell some rubber. He hadn't had a tourist stop for over two years.

"How are we going to keep the *Princess* on the tubes?" my father asked.

We. I liked it when he said *we*.

"I've been sketching," I said. "First, let's get her unloaded."

Sarah helped without being asked. Emily balked at leaving her perch, but soon enough we wheeled the empty *Princess* down to the landing.

I did some more measuring, then went down the shore a ways with a saw. My father helped me cut six small trees—alders, I think; there were hundreds of them along the bank. Each was about wrist thick in diameter, and we cut them eight feet long. After some final measuring, we lashed all six of them to the inner tubes to make a large triangle: the bottom of a raft. Afterward we struggled to lift the empty *Princess* onto the raft frame.

"Sits too high," I said.

"Yes. It'll be tippy and unstable," my father agreed. "We have to take off the wheels."

Sarah groaned as she once again helped us lift the *Princess* back to shore. There I removed the axle nuts and pulled off the wheels. Now we were ready again for final placement. This time the *Princess* fit snugly onto the wooden frame. Using two full rolls of tape and several yards of cord, I made sure she was firmly secured to the raft. As I worked, my father cut two more, longer poles.

"Are you sure about this?" Nat asked as we loaded

the *River Queen*. She did not much like sailing, or the water in general.

"The river's only three feet deep here," I said as my father handed me one of the long poles.

She shrugged and gingerly got on board.

"Now departing, the *Titanic*," Sarah said. She stayed close to the center of the raft; Emily seemed quite happy at the prospect of being on the move again. Maybe in a previous life she was a hood ornament. *"Baaack!"* she called, and with that we shoved off.

Into complete silence.

After all the splashing and scraping and work at the landing, we were suddenly moving slowly downstream with only the tiniest of rippling sounds. My father gave me a thumbs-up as he worked his pole. We didn't really have to push, but only keep ourselves from getting too near the banks where the river curved.

And curve it did, like a slinky toy. Around each bend, ducks or herons and once an eagle lifted up, startled. What a sight we must have been.

The water depth varied from five or more feet to sometimes only a couple of feet; that worried me a bit. My father tested the depth with his pole. "Quarter twain. Half twain. Mark twain," he called. "Actually, I forget which is shallower."

"Did you know that's where Samuel Clemens took his pen name?" my mother said to us.

"Everybody knows that," Sarah said.

Except me.

Deeper into the marsh, which spread out for blocks on either side, the current slowed. Grasses rose up several feet tall on either side. Their pale tops ruffled lightly in a faint breeze.

"First mate, shall we run up the mainsail?" my father said.

"Aye, aye, Captain," I replied. Hoisted by rope and ring, the canvas rattled its top above the marsh grass and caught the breath of wind, and we began to move along steadily again.

We slowly passed through the marsh. The tall, silent, grassy walls meant that we couldn't see out, had to trust the current. Ancient dark logs lay half sunken here and there, and carried lines of little turtles down their backs. From a distance the logs looked like alligators. As we drew closer, the turtles *plook-plook*ed into the water and disappeared into the dark, spongy river bottom. With our poles we had to push against the grassy sedge; beneath the raft, there was nothing to push against. *Soft* *and mucky. Loon shit, I called it.*

We kept moving. We were all silent by the time we rounded a bend and saw the forest again.

"Land ho!" my father called.

"Thank God," my mother said, smiling.

I agreed. Sturdy banks and trees slowly drew close on either side of the river now. Here the river bottom became lighter, sandier; minnows flashed in the deeper, green pockets, and the sudden shadows of larger fish (bass? northern pike?) arrowed away from the *River Queen*. Tall bushes lined the banks and drooped with clusters of berries still green but turning to pink.

"High-bush cranberries," I said suddenly.

My family stared. At first they didn't see them.

"There," I pointed.

As we passed through forest, the river narrowed further. Both my father and I could push off nicely from the firm riverbanks.

Where I lived, a good man could jump clear across the Mississippi. . . .

My only worry was that the river would become too narrow for the raft. I began to squint into the forest on either side as the river narrowed further. A stretch of tall maple trees formed a canopy, a dusty green tunnel, just ahead.

Crossed the river in my car, kept it hid in the trees. . . .

Was there another bridge nearby? I kept looking. "We're not far now," I said.

"I don't see anything," Sarah said.

"Me neither," Nat said.

As we scanned the banks, peering into the trees for sight of a cabin, the canopy above gradually grew lower. And at the moment I remembered our mainmast, it was too late. The raft rocked in one shuddering motion—there was a sharp snapping sound—and we were all pitched into the shallow, chilly water. One moment silence, then chaos as we splashed and scrambled to rescue our suitcases and other gear. *"Baack! Baack!"* Emily called.

"Pitch everything up onto the bank," I shouted. And I was amazed: We acted so fast—sort of like high-speed cartoon characters—that hardly anything got wet—except us.

"What happened?" Sarah sputtered. Emily, on shore, shook off a spray of water like a wet dog.

"The mast hit an overhead branch," I said. "It's broken." I couldn't believe I had let this happen.

"Not a branch," my father said. "Look."

Stretching bank to bank several feet above us, and nearly invisible with overgrown branches and leaves, was a thick wire. Both ends disappeared into the foliage.

"It's a power line!" Nat said, fear suddenly in her voice.

"No. It's like a fence, or a cable of some kind," I said.

"Whatever. We're still wet and the mast is broken," Sarah said. "Now what do we do?" She was very close to blubbering.

"Let me lower the rest of the mast; then we'll reload our gear," my father said.

"Yes. I'll be right back," I said, my eyes on the cable.

"Don't get lost!" Nat called as I scrambled up the riverbank, which rose up toward the big wire. Soon I could grab hold. It was taut, about an inch in diameter, and thick with ash. However, underneath was a black film—grease—that rubbed on my fingers. Why would there be grease on a wire? I pushed through thick brush and leaves to see where it was anchored.

And suddenly there sat a small cart. A cart hung on the cable by two small iron wheels. The cable itself was secured to what looked like a length of railroad iron driven who knew how deep into the ground. I examined the little cart again.

The car!

I began to laugh out loud.

"Miles—what's the matter?" Nat shrilled from below.

Didn't run on gasoline, it ran on itself. I couldn't stop laughing.

"Miles, come back, you're scaring us," my mother called.

"Okay," I called. I untied the little car—its rotted tether rope fell away in chunks, but the car itself, the wheels, and the cable were solid enough to last another hundred years. "Here I come," I called, and pushed off.

As I burst through the leaves high above the river in my cable car, the shouting and the scrambling below really should have been videotaped. Emily went *"Baack! Baack!"* and bolted for cover; so did the rest of my family.

"Whoa!" my father said. He had grabbed a long pole as if to defend himself.

"Whoa is right!" I called. I was picking up speed— the cable ran slightly downhill—and not far beyond a shroud of green leaves on the opposite side, the car hit hard. I kept going, flipping at least once and landing with a *whooph!* on the dirt bank.

"Miles—Miles! Are you all right?"

I struggled to catch my breath—had the wind knocked out of me. Couldn't speak. My parents scrambled up the bank and burst through the brush. I managed to at least sit up before they arrived.

"All right . . . all right," I wheezed.

"That will teach you," Sarah said; she stood there, hands on her hips.

"I agree," Nat said.

"This is it, don't you see? This is Mr. Kurz's car. We're here," I said hoarsely.

They all looked around.

"I don't see any cabin," my mother said.

To my supreme annoyance it was Sarah who took one step farther up the bank, held aside some leaves, and yelled, "There it is! I found it!"

CHAPTER EIGHTEEN

MEMORY BOOK

I BROUGHT UP THE REAR, though not for long. My mother drew up short; I stumbled against her. "That's it?" she whispered.

I stepped around her. A few yards ahead, facing south and dug partially into the bank of the hill, was a little wooden cabin. And a vandalized cabin at that. The front door hung askew. One of two front windows was broken. Two rough-hewn chairs lay tipped over on the porch.

"Somebody's been here," my father said.

"Maybe, maybe not." I led the way.

Vines coiled and trailed around the posts of the little front porch. Grass poked up here and there through the board floor like a botched haircut. My father and I mounted the steps. They were sturdy enough.

"We'll wait down here," my mother said.

At the sound of our boots near the front door, a striped ball of fur dashed between us, leaped past Nat and Sarah—who shrieked—and scuttled away down the riverbank.

"Raccoon!" I said. "They're harmless."

I examined the broken door. There were large, raking claw marks where some creature had torn away enough wood to loosen the hinges.

"Bear," I said softly to my father.

His eyes widened.

"Not here now," I said. "There's no fresh tracks anywhere around."

"Will he come back?"

"Maybe not." I peered inside. As my eyes adjusted to the dim light inside the shack, I could see the damage. The bear had trashed the place. Tables and chairs were tipped. Cupboards were ripped off the wall. Canisters were scratched and clawed. Jam jars were broken and emptied. The raccoon, and then mice, had finished the job. Everything wooden was gnawed on. The corners of tables and chairs were rounded off and splintery. A wooden bed frame tilted from a short leg.

Then I heard a scratching noise at the same moment as my father yelled and leaped through the door.

"There's something in there, Miles!" he shouted. "Watch out!"

In the corner, staring dully at me, sat a small dumpy animal with beady eyes and long coarse fur, almost like feather vanes.

Stupidest animal in the woods. Can't run, can't hide, can't do anything right. But that's why he has quills. Everybody leaves him alone.

"Porcupine," I called. I found an old broom. "Shoo!" I said.

His back arched up and his floppy tail waved menacingly, but then he turned and lumbered toward the door. There were various shrieks and exclamations outside.

"He's harmless," I called.

My family gave the porcupine a wide berth as he passed by on his way back to the forest.

"Safe now," I called.

As I continued to inspect Mr. Kurz's cabin, my family

slowly gathered just inside the doorway.

My mother let out a breath. "We can't live here." Her voice wilted to a whisper.

Sarah was speechless.

"It's a little messy," I said. But I didn't care about that. I examined the ceiling, which was fairly low, under eight feet, and made lower still by the heavy round log beams that stretched across; however, there were no stains or other signs of leakage from the roof. The walls and the floors were solid. A barrel stove, its pipe knocked down, sat ready at the rear; a rusty wooden cookstove waited near the pantry.

"It's not the mess, it's the size," my mother said.

I looked around. All in all the cabin was about sixteen feet square. A one-man, one-room cabin.

"All four of us can't live here for a winter," Sarah said. "We'd go crazy."

"It's definitely not Birch Bay," I said.

"What are these big scrape marks all over?" Sarah asked.

I glanced at my father and he at me. "Various-sized rodents," I answered. "But they're all gone now."

"I'm sleeping in the tent tonight, that's for sure," Sarah answered as she looked around.

Outside, I followed the path toward the shed. Low skinny bushes with small pointy leaves lined the path. Some of them had clusters of gray berries. As my boot knocked against one little bush, the gray dust fell away.

"Blueberries," I said. I knelt and picked a couple.

"Are you sure?" my mother said quickly.

I nodded and popped them into my mouth. "They taste just like blueberry syrup."

Sarah cautiously picked a single berry and tasted it. "It's true," she said to my mother.

But I was headed to the shed. Its door, too, had been clawed and battered, but inside, the contents were intact. The walls were hung with sledgehammers, wood-splitting mauls, axes, Swede saws, crosscut saws, ice saws, ice tongs, block and tackle, chains, and tools I could not name. Many appeared to be for handling logs—rolling them, peeling them, notching them. In the corner was a large pedal grindstone for sharpening blades of all kinds. There was even a pail full of rusty nails. The shed was like a museum of hand tools from a previous century.

"Cool!" I murmured.

"What's there?" my father said from behind me.

I stepped aside so he could see for himself; that's

when I saw, through the brush, the overgrown sawmill complete with piles of slab wood and rough boards.

"Everything we need," I replied.

We camped that evening down by the river. Mother and Sarah found the trashed cabin too depressing to look at—let alone consider living there. I built a campfire, and we had a decent supper of rice and pasta and cheese and tea. As we ate, a fish splashed in the small pool where the river bent deeper into the trees. Emily, on a tether, grazed contentedly on tufts of grass on the bank. Nobody said much. Nobody mentioned the cabin.

"Well, gang," my father finally ventured.

"Well what?" Sarah said, not looking up from the red coals.

"What do you think?"

"About what?" Sarah said with exasperation.

"About the cabin, I'd guess?" my mother said.

I was silent.

"I have to say, it would be tough for all of us to live here all winter," my father ventured.

"I agree," I replied.

Sarah looked up at me with surprise.

"But it's not winter yet," I said. "Not for three

months, four if we're lucky."

"Meaning?" Sarah said.

"As we all agreed, we could do worse than camp on the Mississippi for the summer," I said.

They looked around at our little river valley.

"True," my mother said.

Sarah shrugged in agreement.

"What I'm saying is, give me a couple of months to work on the cabin, and then we can decide whether or not to stay."

"You can fix it up all you want, but it's still not going to be any bigger," Sarah said.

"Maybe, maybe not," I replied. I let my eyes flicker to the sturdy trees that rose up all around us, a whole forest of them; I already had a plan, but I didn't want to say much right now. It's never a good thing to talk a lot about what you're going to do. Just start on it and keep on it until you finish.

"I don't want you to go to a lot of work for nothing," Mother said to me.

I shrugged, and with a stick pushed at a red ember. "That's what you said once about the *Ali Princess.*"

She was silent for a moment. "That's true. I shouldn't have doubted you, Miles."

"Me neither," my father said softly.

I looked up. Across the campfire my parents were sitting close to each other and smiling. At me.

"Maybe things in the city will improve over the summer," Sarah said with sudden optimism. "We'll keep track of the news, and when we know that it's safe, we can go back. Back home." Her voice broke slightly at the end.

"It's possible," my father said.

We all fell silent. Just then, low and dusty orange rays of sunlight leaned around the trees and lit up the river. It was sundown in the valley.

"So we'll stay here this summer, right?" I said.

There was another brief silence. We all looked at one another.

"Yes."

"Okay."

"Yes."

"Unanimous, then," I said.

"But I'll warn you right now," Sarah said, "it would take a small miracle for me to live in that shack this winter."

"I hear you," I said easily. In the quiet moment that followed, a fish splashed in the shady corner pool; I thought about finding my fishing pole and making a couple of casts, but he would be there tomorrow.

"You know, I think I'll turn in," my mother said sleepily.

"Me too," my father said.

My mother hugged me—and then, awkwardly, so did my father. I hugged him back.

After Sarah secured Emily, she too headed into the tent. "Don't stay up too late, Memory Boy." It was her way, too, of apologizing for doubting me.

"I won't."

When my parents and Sarah were in their tents, I stretched out by the fire and watched the stars come out and listened to night sounds. An owl went *"whoo-whoo-whoo"*; the campfire whispered. Then, when I closed my eyes, I heard Mr. Kurz's voice:

Burn too much pine in your stove and you're asking for trouble. Creosote tar builds up in the pipe, and the next thing you know, you've got a chimney fire. . . .

Upstream there's plenty of wild rice. Listen for mallards—the ducks that quack loudest—they'll tell you where to look. There's plenty of rice for everyone. Cook it dry and slow when you parch it. In winter boil it in water with a little salt. It's better than potatoes any day. . . .

I suddenly opened my eyes and looked around—but there was only Emily, the tents, and the campfire. So I closed my eyes again and listened to every story Mr. Kurz had told me. Some of them had parts missing because I hadn't listened well; others came back whole. They flowed out of my memory like a river.

If you need venison, take a small deer. One that might not make it through the winter. Find a deer trail, make a little brush blind twenty yards off it, and wait there. Keep the wind in your face and stay quiet as a tree. The deer will come. Aim for the neck. One good shot is all you need. Dressing out a deer is messy, but don't worry about the gut pile. The fox will clean it up overnight. . . .

Living in the woods is like swimming in deep water. If you fight against it, if you're scared of it, you'll drown. But if you learn to trust it, to take what the land gives you, you'll be okay. In fact you'll be more than okay—you'll be fine.

I suddenly opened my eyes: It was almost dark, and there was one last thing to do.

I eased my backpack from the tent, and from it took out the small, well-sealed bottle. It felt lighter than ever.

I went to the river and knelt there. Carefully I unscrewed the lid. Before me the water was blue-purple now, and darker still where it curled into the dusky forest. With a flick of my wrist, I tossed Mr. Kurz's ashes onto the water. For a moment they rode high, then sank in a swirl of gray. I watched their lighter shape drift on the current, turn, spin—almost like dancing—and then he was gone.

eXTRAS

MEMORY

BOY

A Q&A with Will Weaver

Miles's Guide to Survival

An exclusive look of the sequel, *The Survivors*

A Q&A with Will Weaver

You live in Northern Minnesota and are an avid outdoorsman. What survival skills have you developed from living in the country?

Having grown up on a farm and as an outdoors kid, a lot of lessons from my father and grandfather have rubbed off on me. For example, how to make a fire, identify animal tracks, and catch a fish. It's reassuring in a primitive sort of way to know that I could survive—and provide food for my family—if there was some huge calamity like Miles and his family endure.

As a former teacher, do you have a memory as sharp as Miles? What are your tips for retaining all of that information we learn in class?

No way do I have a Miles Newell kind of memory! But like most of us, my brain holds the important things and lets the trivial stuff slip through the cracks. In terms of retaining information from class, I like the term "take away." As in, okay, what were the key points that I should take away from that class or that meeting? If we write down the "take away" in note form, all the better.

Miles is skeptical about the "Adopt a Geezer" project, but he ends up learning a lot—and it helps save him and his family when they need it most. Who have you learned something vital from? How did it help you in a particular situation?

I've learned the most from observing and keeping quiet, at least to start with. They say we seldom learn much when we're talking. But vital stuff? Hmmmm, good question. I think I've learned as much from reading as from real people. Reading lets us try on other people's lives and learn from their mistakes without actually making those mistakes. Is that a good deal or what?!

Which book or character affected you the most as a teen and made you think about or act on something differently?

We all have books that strike us like meteors, that come out of nowhere and rock our world. Mine was an unlikely one called *The Honey Badger*, an adult novel by Robert Ruark. The story was about a playboy-type fellow, a big game hunter but also smooth with women and at home in the bars of New York City and other worldly watering holes. The novel struck me because its story was so *very* far from my life on a small farm in northern Minnesota. It was like, "Whoa—people actually live like that?" The lifestyle of the main character seemed unimaginably sophisticated and cool.

A lot of natural disasters have happened since *Memory Boy* was first published—Hurricane Katrina and many others, tsunamis, and major earthquakes. Did a real disaster inspire this story?

Memory Boy came from two sources: a family trip to Yellowstone National Park in Montana when I was small, and the Mount Saint Helens eruption in Washington State in 1980 when I was an adult. As a boy at Yellowstone, I was fascinated by its geothermal activity—the enormous power just below the surface. (And by the way, Yellowstone could eventually be the volcano that makes *Memory Boy* and *The Survivors* seem very real.) But Mount Saint Helens and its eruption was equally fascinating. A fiction writer by then, I asked myself a short question: "What if?" What if Mount Saint Helens had been ten times as big? Or a hundred times as big? What would the

4

effect be on our climate? On us? The answer, it was clear to me, would make a great novel.

Miles and his family are forced to flee their house in Minneapolis in the wake of the volcanic eruption, on the *Ali Princess*. Where would you go if you had to evacuate? And how would you get there?
Evacuations take many forms, but most often people simply have to walk—in some cases for many, many miles. And few people are prepared. I'm not some kind of survivalist fanatic, but I do think we could all benefit from at least *thinking* about a "worst-case" scenario. In fact, let's hear some survival ideas from Miles!

Miles's Guide to Survival
Learn how to get through the toughest situations— straight from Miles

You don't think it's going to happen to you. A disaster, I mean. One day you're rolling along down the highway of life, and then out of nowhere looms the texting driver. Or the tornado. Or, in my family's case, the volcanoes. Old Man Kurz warned me about "hard times." He said they'd come again and he was right. Luckily I was mostly paying attention. My family got through it, but some people didn't. They just freaked. Well let me tell you, that's not the way to survive. And if I had to go through it again, I'd be way better prepared.

There's one thing for sure I'd have on hand: a "Go Bag." That is, a backpack or duffel bag stashed somewhere, like under your bed, which you can grab and go if you have to leave. Here's what I'd have in it:

- A multipurpose, heavy-duty, camping-type pocketknife. You know, the kind with ten different blades, including a sharp one to defend yourself or skin a rabbit, along with a can-opener blade, a screwdriver, etc. A good pocket-knife can save your life in many ways.
- A change of clothes, including a poncho for wet weather. You need to stay dry and warm (disasters seldom include perfect summer weather).
- A pair of good hiking boots and some wool socks (you're going to be walking, trust me)
- Some light rope or cord (there are a million uses for rope, including stringing up a tarp to make a shelter or for snaring a squirrel to eat)

6

- Matches in a sealed plastic bag (you don't want wet matches)
- Some kind of mini-flashlight, and an extra battery for your cell phone
- A compass to tell you what direction you need to go (the idea is to get away from the disaster)

This leads me to another sad fact. Most people don't know their cardinal directions. I'm talking about north, south, east, and west. Believe me, you need to know these things. Can you give directions to other people? Follow a map? Most people depend on global position satellites (GPS) and some annoying voice that tells them where to turn. But when the grid goes down, all these people will be screwed. They'll be wandering around like zombies.

And one last general survival tip: Let's say you belong to some club or group, and you're going on a summer canoe or camping trip. You have a parent or a guide who's the leader, and off you go down the river or into the bush. Well, let me tell you, adults know way less than you think they do. So why trust them with your life? You should have your own map, your own compass, your own information, your own survival gear. Because what if your great adult leader suddenly tips over with a heart attack, or gets struck by lightning (which happens all the time in Minnesota where I live). Then what do you do? You save the day, of course, by being the cool one. The Prepared One.

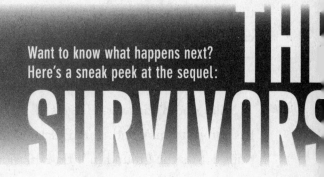

Want to know what happens next?
Here's a sneak peek at the sequel:

THE SURVIVORS

SARAH

THE SKY IS NOT FALLING. At least not today. No yellow haze, no volcano dust—it's a hot, late August afternoon with a mostly blue sky. Life feels almost normal, which means that Sarah and her brother, Miles, are arguing.

"—just saying, how many kids would go to school if they didn't have to?" Miles asks. He stops sawing to look at her.

"Lots," Sarah replies. She's watching him work, which always annoys him.

"Not me, that's for sure!" Miles says. He touches a finger to the bright handsaw blade. Tests its sharpness.

"You're still in school."

"Alternative school—which means I don't have to *go* there," Miles replies, turning to grab another board. "I can do my class work at home. You should try it."

"And why would I want to stay *home*?" Sarah says sarcastically as she glances at their cabin in the woods.

Miles doesn't answer. He gets all adult-like when he has a tool in his hand. Sarah kicks a pinecone, which skips across the ground in little explosions of fine gray ash—or tephra, as scientists call the stuff. "Maybe I like regular school," she says.

"You never did before," Miles says, bending again to his work. The shiny handsaw blade goes *RASS!—RASS!* back and forth against the wood. His tanned arms glisten with sweat, and the piney sawdust odor is strong but does not cover his stinky smell. "Back home—" *RASS!—* "hated—" *RASS!—* "skipped—" *RASS!—* "the time."

"Not all the time. And we weren't homeless then," Sarah says.

Miles quickly stops sawing. He points the shiny blade toward their cabin. "We are *not* homeless."

Her gaze follows his to the little shack tucked into the pines. The trees behind are shaggy gray with the volcano dust that coats everything, and that has totally screwed up her life. Less than two months ago she lived in Wayzata, a western suburb of Minneapolis. Her family's big house in the cul-de-sac, her life of hanging out with her seventh-grade friends at school and at the Cinnabon in Southdale and the Mall of America and Valley Fair—all of that now feels like a dream. Either a dream or else she is stuck inside a cheesy disaster movie about a suburban family trying to survive an environmental disaster.

"Yeah. Some home," Sarah says. "It looks like it was built for trolls."

"Hey, think what it looked like when we first arrived," Miles says.

Sarah is silent.

"Trashed," Miles continues. "Now we've got gaslights, a front porch—Mr. Kurz would be proud."

"He's dead," she says sarcastically. Miles pauses to give her a glare but doesn't go off on her.

"Well, we're not dead," he says, "and thanks to him we at least have a safe place to stay."

Mr. Kurz—another character from the bad movie she's stuck in. He was an old guy whom Miles had met at a nursing home in Minneapolis during his ninth-grade oral-history project, or "interview a geezer," as Miles called it then. The old man had a crazy story about living in a cabin hidden in the north woods all his life; Miles was crazy enough to believe him; and their parents, Art and Natalie, were crazy enough to let Miles bring them all here. Then again, it wasn't as if they had much choice.

"It's great living in the woods by the river," Miles says. "Why would anyone want to leave?"

"Let's see," Sarah says, "a real school might actually have kids my age? Plus my cell phone won't work here. I can't call any of my friends back home."

"What friends?" Mile says. "And anyway, all those suburban fake-Goth losers you hung around with are going to be hunting rats or looking for roadkill to eat."

"Shut up, Miles!" she says quickly.

Miles does, which is his small way of apologizing.

"Plus a school has things like flush toilets," Sarah continues, "and hot water that comes out of faucets?"

"Our outhouse works fine," Miles says, not bothering to look up. "No pipes, no electricity—we're totally green. And what's wrong with cooking on a woodstove and washing in the river?"

"You tell me."

He stops to stare.

She pinches her nose. "I hate to say it, but you stink. Really bad."

Miles hoists his right arm and smells his pit. "I don't smell nothing."

"'Anything,'" she says. Since they'd arrived at the cabin, Miles's grammar and hygiene had slipped big-time. He hardly ever washes—never brushes his teeth. His hair has gotten longer, and now that he's getting older, his skinny chest is growing furry with dark hair. Every day he looks more like a wild animal.

Miles straightens up. "I stink? Really?" he says, now faking genuine concern; he sniffs first one armpit, then the other. He steps closer. "Are you sure?"

"Miles, no," Sarah says, edging away.

He fakes a growl and leaps forward to grab her. Sarah shrieks. He's so sweaty and slick from his carpentry work that she twists out of his grasp and races off toward the river. He waves his arms like a crazy man, and his hairy armpits chase her like two owls. Laughing, she runs down the path toward the river. Behind her, Emily, their goat, begins to *"Baaack!"* in alarm.

"Don't worry, Emily—I'll be back!" Sarah shouts over her shoulder. She makes a running jump into the water, hoping that Miles will leap in after her. It would be a service to the family.

But Miles skids to a stop at the riverbank. "Sorry," he says, "I got to keep working. Winter is coming, and anyway, you smell, too—like a goat."

"I do not!" she shouts.

"Goat Girl!" Miles teases.

She punches water toward him but it falls short, then swears at him for real.

"Sarah? Miles?" their mom calls from back on the front porch. "Everything all right?"

"You're in trouble now," Sarah says, emerging from the river.

"No I'm not." Miles quickly heads back to the yard.

As Sarah trudges, sopping wet, up the short trail and into the yard, her mother waits on the front porch, arms crossed. "Okay, what's going on?"

"Miles did it. He chased me," Sarah says, pointing to him.

Miles looks around innocently. "She's obsessing on toilets and showers again," he says, and shrugs.

"That's enough, Miles," Nat says. "I don't care who did what—just stop!" Their mother is small and with dark-blue eyes; and a red do-rag covers her curly dark brown hair. Art appears in the doorway and takes out one earbud.

"What's going on?" he asks. He's only a little taller than Nat, and has wispy curls turning gray over his ears; he shades his eyes against the hazy sunlight—he's an indoor kind of man, a musician, drummer for a jazz band, and a totally urban guy.

"Nothing," Sarah says.

"I'm so sick of these two bickering and fighting," Nat says to him.

"Listen to your mother," their father says.

"So what? Are you going to ground me?" Sarah asks her parents. "Take away my cell phone and credit card? No trips to the mall for a week?"

"Very funny," her mother says.

They are all silent for a moment.

"We just need . . . to pull together," her mother says. "Okay?"

"All right, all right!" Sarah says with annoyance. She isn't used to this new family teamwork motto. She used to have essentially no parents. Her dad was on the road all the time with his group, and her mother was busy with her literary clients—and it was just fine that way. Now they're like the *Little House on the Prairie* family—or more like *Little House in the Big Woods*: Everybody's home all the time. "Just tell me again why we're living here?" Sarah says.

Everyone knows it's a rhetorical question, but Miles isn't done pushing her buttons. "Where to start?" he says sarcastically. "Do you sorta remember when the volcanoes didn't stop erupting, how we had to wait longer and longer in line at gas stations? How fights would break out if somebody took more than five gallons? And how after about a year of volcanic dust in the air, the plants barely grew anymore, and all the grocery store shelves had big bare spots? All the 'temporarily out of stock' signs?"

"That the best you can do, Memory Boy?"

"Or how about the family down the road that was tied up and beaten by looters looking for food?" Miles continues.

"What family?" Sarah asks.

"Exactly," Miles answers. "I wasn't supposed to tell you—not that you were paying attention anyway—because it might have scared you. The looters did some really bad things to the mother and daughter, too."

"Shut up!" Sarah says.

"Stop! Right now!" Nat calls to both of them.

There's a long silence.

"Did you really have to do that?" Nat asks Miles.

Miles doesn't answer, which makes Nat let out a long breath. "Oh, Miles," she begins.

"Forget about that," Miles says abruptly. "We're here now. And I thought—finally—we were all on the same page."

"And what page is that?" Sarah asks. She tries to sound sarcastic.

"We get out of the city and stay out until it's safe to go home," Miles answers. "Here at least we have enough to eat." There is no hesitation in his voice.

Sarah and her parents are silent.

"We voted, remember?!" Miles asks, trying to keep anger from his voice.

Sarah is silent.

"Okay. Then let's get with the program, people!" Miles says. He heads back to his work.

Sarah's father disappears back inside the cabin. Emily continues to hop and fidget, so Sarah goes over and gives her a handful of grass. Emily nuzzles her long nose, wide-set eyes, and bumpy head through two slats in the wooden corral fence, and Sarah scratches her head.

"It's all right. Things are fine," she lies.

When Emily calms down, Sarah heads back to the river for a real swim; the river is the place she goes to get away from her family.

Among some trees on the riverbank, she takes her damp bathing suit from a tree limb and changes out of her wet clothes. Falls back into the cool, flowing water. Just when she's starting to relax, her mother appears and sits down on the bank like a lifeguard.

Sarah ignores her. Rolls over on her back and floats.

"I know this is tough," her mother begins.

Sarah says nothing.

"None of your friends are around. And we spend way more time together as a family than we used to," her mother adds. "We're all adjusting to that."

Sarah blurts, "Since when did Miles become the boss of our family?"

"He's not the boss," Nat says.

"Well he acts like it."

Nat is silent.

"Is it true—about that family?" Sarah asks.

"Yes. Miles just wants to keep us safe and get us through this—these *times*."

Sarah spits a fountain-like mouthful of river water. " 'These times,' " she says sarcastically.

Her mother shrugs. "Every generation has something—some issue to deal with, like a war or a depression. Yours will be the volcanoes. Think of the great stories you'll have to tell your own kids—"

"I thought we were talking about Miles."

"Okay, yes. Miles gets pretty intense about things," Nat says. "Especially about our cabin because it belonged to Mr. Kurz—"

"I know all that stuff," Sarah interrupts.

"But what we didn't know was how much he and Miles bonded," her mother continues. "They spent a lot of time together. I think he became a grandfather Miles never had."

"Or maybe the father he never had?" Sarah asks.

"Don't be cruel," her mother says sharply.

Sarah doesn't reply.

"But in some ways you're right," her mother says. "We had our family issues. Maybe this time together is a gift. Try to look at it that way."

A small dragonfly lands on the bridge of Sarah's nose—she crosses her eyes and tries to focus on its cellophane wings, its bug eyes; but it's too close. The dragonfly's feet tickle her skin as it launches itself back up in the air; she itches her nose. "I hate it here!" she says. "I wish we were back at Birch Bay—our own cabin. That's where we're supposed to be living."

"Let's not talk about that," her mother says.

"We're going to have to someday," Sarah says.

Her mother does not reply.

"Okay, let's not," Sarah says. She takes in a big breath of air and lets herself sink to the bottom of the Mississippi River—which is less dramatic than it sounds. They are only twenty miles from the headwaters at Lake Itasca, and here the Mississippi is only waist deep. It's narrow enough to leap across in spots. A cold, clear stream with small rocks and tiny shells on the sandy bottom, and the deeper pools where the river bends. Underwater, she opens her eyes. Pretends she's a fish. Minnows with horizontal stripes and half-transparent bodies flicker by. A silvery shell the size of an ear glints like mother of pearl, and she grabs it. Underwater there's no sound except for her own heartbeat—and the muffled *"Baaack!"* of Emily. She sounds far away—where Sarah would like to be.

She stays down a long time, hoping that her mother will think she has drowned. It wouldn't be the worst way to go, sort of a cool, drifty death with all the dust washed away. She imagines shouting, splashing, hands reaching down to save her.

When she spews air and resurfaces, her mother is halfway back to the cabin. Clutching her shell, she emerges from the river, grabs a towel hung over the side of Miles's old raft, and dries off. She changes behind a little board screen that she made herself. On the way up the path, she yanks up a handful of thin grass, shakes off the dust, and carries it back to the corral. A nice treat for Emily.

Emily, with her soft, droopy ears, her Roman nose, her wide brown eyes and musky smell that Sarah has come to love. Emily was a "free parting gift" from the squatters occupying the Newell family's real lake cabin— where her family *should* be living right now. Birch Bay was their destination when they'd left Minneapolis: a cozy summer cabin near Brainerd that had belonged to her grandparents. The place they always went to on summer weekends. But this time when they got to Birch Bay it was occupied by squatters. A family with kids and a biker and his wife. *You folks are gonna have to move on. It's a dog-eat-dog world nowadays,* the creepy biker, big Danny, had said; and since he was a big guy with a big gun, and his wife was related to the local sheriff who would protect them, the Newell family had to move on. It was her family's most humiliating moment ever—especially for her father.

"But the bad people you came from don't make you a bad goat!" Sarah says.

"Baaack, baack!" replies Emily.

Sarah snuggles against her, but Emily is fidgety. Nervous. Her eyes keep turning toward the woods. Toward Miles, who is working across the clearing.

"What's wrong?" Sarah murmurs.

"Baaack, baaack!"

Sarah holds out more grass, which Emily munches on. But she keeps looking around.

"Lend a hand anytime!" Miles calls; he lifts another board onto his sawhorses.

"I'm feeding Emily."

Miles mutters something she can't hear.

"Look what I found in the river," she says. She holds up the shell. The inside curve looks like a pearl; by tilting it she can reflect weak sunlight.

"Clam," Miles says. "Actually a clam shell. The clam inside got ate by an otter or a mink."

"'Eaten,'" she says.

"That's what I said," Miles replies, and keeps sawing.

She gives Emily another handful of dusty grass—

and when she stands up, she sees a dog watching them from the edge of the woods. A dog the same color as the brush. All grays and browns and tans, like oak leaves. She squints to see him better, but suddenly he's not there.

It was definitely a dog. An old one, too. A gray muzzle and square head, which is how she noticed him—his large head with its up-slanted eyes. And a tattered part of a collar hanging down—she's sure about that. Somebody's lost dog.

She glances again at Miles, who remains intent on his boards. His shotgun leans nearby. She doesn't say anything about the old dog.

The long-anticipated sequel to
MEMORY BOY

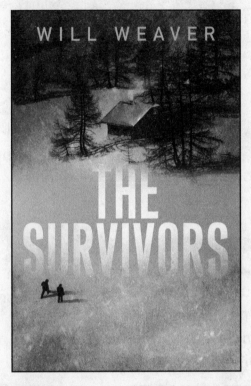

TWO YEARS AGO, the ash started falling like gray snow.
The volcanoes had erupted . . . and changed the world. Now,
in order to survive, Sarah and Miles must change with it.

Will Weaver delivers an extraordinary sequel to *Memory Boy*,
showing that several basic instincts lie deep within us all:
love, fear, and the desire to survive.